UNTETHERED

JOHN BOWIE

RED DOG
UK

Published by RED DOG PRESS 2020

Second Edition
First Edition published by Silverwood Books 2017

Paperback ISBN 978-1-913331-81-8

Ebook ISBN 978-1-913331-82-5

www.reddogpress.co.uk

For Ellie

PRAISE FOR UNTETHERED

'Bowie's dark, hard-edged crime novel inaugurates a promising series.'—**Publishers Weekly**

'Dark, hard-edged crime noir.'—**Publishers Weekly**

'Noir fans will find a lot to like.'—**BookLife**

'Bowie's writing is lyrical, moody, funny and as gritty as hell...like a British blend of Jim Thompson and Nelson Algren.'—**Paul D. Brazill, author of Guns of Brixton**

'I would definitely recommend this crime novel and John Bowie as an author, and look forward to reading his next book.'—**Amanda Brightman**

'It's a loopy surreal fever dream of a novel, a dark, disorienting Möbius strip of people and places that are not always what they seem.'—**'The Thrilling Detective'**

'...its pages are packed full of deceit, human depravity and surprisingly dark humour.'—**STORGY.com**

[un·teth·er]

un·teth·ered, un·teth·er·ing, un·teth·ers

1. To unfasten the tether of or release from a tether.
2. To disconnect: An opinion that was untethered to reality.
3. To free from restraints: The experience untethered his imagination.

PROLOGUE

I thought I'd lost everything, but I hadn't quite. Not yet. I realised that, bound to a chair in a depressing hotel room. Dust from the drawn curtains was caught in mid-air by a yellow hue from outside as time froze. What remained of me was between the blades of a pair of bolt croppers. They were razor-sharp, poised. About to snap shut. Without hope, I was like a lost wilting butterfly resting under a steamroller about to move.

I took her bait, chose to be there. A master puppeteer, she'd played me, and them too. She had a well-honed game. But I wasn't who they thought. With empty pockets and no future, it was if they looked to rob me of my pockets themselves, and with it my hopes of a new life. With only the bottom half of me laid bare for the blades, no one could see my torso: the ghosts, scars, service tattoo. There are wars in the rivers of those aged cuts, burns and holes. If they could only see — they would think again.

If it was down to me, I'd pass out, before it came: the blood. And, not wake up... They wouldn't give me a choice. When I woke, there would be much more blood. Running black, like lost rivers in the moonlight.

My therapist told me to write it all out. That it would help me come to terms with the memories of the wars, pain and suffering. My notebook held everything that brought me to them. It was an arm's length away. If they would just pick it up, they'd see... They have the wrong man.

If they read that notebook, it would make clear the descending darkness that had brought me to them.

1

No Future. That's what the graffiti on a building opposite my flat says in blood red and childish scribbles. Below, a stencil image of a sad young girl holds the O as a balloon on a string. It's a dark spring month of 1998, my twenty-seventh birthday and I've been given another non-descript corporate office job to hide myself away in, starting tomorrow. Let's just say witness protection was getting me down, and I'm drunk, bored and alone.

Most evenings I find myself with my feet fixed to the same spot, squinting my eyes through the windows of the run-down flat on Lower Park Row in Bristol. I gaze out over the rooftops whilst imagining the evening's orange lights are flames rebounding off the sky and the drunken screams echoing below are people trapped and burning. The city's soul is on fire and touching the glass, I can't imagine the flames ever reaching me.

I sit myself down at the big table in front of the tall windows and stare out into the night again. Using a glass has become a waste of time and I now drink directly from a wine bottle. I pick at the label and occasionally attempt to write something in a white Moleskine notebook, given to me by my therapist, the contents of which have been going nowhere almost as long as I have, fully representing my state of mind. Which is what she asked for in the first place.

An Irish couple upstairs have been shouting at each other on and off for the past three hours and are starting up again. I hadn't thought to buy a TV or radio, so have nothing to turn the volume up on to drown the noise of them out. So instead, I take the last hit from the first bottle of cheap wine of the evening and move towards the second.

'You fucking loose bitch, why?' the man yells, rattling the exposed light bulb that dangles, shade-less, from my ceiling.

'You bastard!' she screeches back, vibrating the curtain-less window panes in front of me.

'Happy Birthday,' I whisper. 'Happy Birthday!' and I down half of the second bottle, write a line in the notebook and listen to the relentless shouting coming from above. I decide to move back through to the bathroom at the back of the flat. I rub the red stains from my lips and prepare to go out. Or maybe that was all the preparation I'd need?

Leaning on the sink and looking at myself in the mirror, I contemplate that I'm the only person I can look straight in the eye for any duration. I look for a feeling or a thought; anything from the real me left behind. Searching for a hook from this new person and identity I've been given by the authorities; those assumed to know better. My past and real me wait to get pulled through to the surface and breathe life again.

The basin is half full and I splash water on my face, thinking of what or who the night could bring if I head out into the darkness. Then I walk back through to the front room and survey the city lights spread out ahead, trying to entice me. It isn't working, but I go to leave anyway.

Whilst opening my door, I hear the door to the flat above also opening and the arguing couple's consoled murmurs build in a soft undertone of words exchanged until the inevitable hard angst-filled slam of the door that follows. I guess by him, closing the dialogue down—an attempted last word of an argument, made physical with a door and frame. I put on my old black jacket from the hook on the back of the door. I back myself up and close it again slowly and quietly, hoping to hear their footsteps leave down the stairwell ahead of me.

I re-open it, but mistime the situation as they have wandered slowly down the stairs making up with each other a little more, and are now just on the hall landing, in front of me. His arm is around her slight frame and she has long, deep cherry-red hair. They look up at me from their huddled slow-moving mass and cast me a fake neighbourly smile. Her eyes are still red from crying and his too—with rage. They look down on me from all angles. A couple, near sober and dressed like they care and I can see they've spent as long on their mutual appearance as I have looking vacantly out into the darkness.

To them, I must stench out the hallway with my desperate drunken solitude and lack of self. Their mistake is that they're possibly thinking it might be something of my personality, just the natural course of things. Fact is I'm between my own real life and fictions dreamt up by the authorities right now. I'm nothing to these vacuous idiots that have spent all day fucking and preening themselves, before arguing about who gets to use the hair straighteners next. To them, I'm a nothing man. Look into my eyes though, and you'll see the flames of yesterday—someday maybe they'll look to the future—not yet though, not yet.

'Alright? Off out?' he says.

'Alright. Yes, something like that,' I say, saving myself from the unlikely event of them inviting themselves along by not giving anything away or showing any interest in what they're doing.

'We didn't disturb you, did we?' she asks, and looks at her

feet, submissively.

'No, no, I just turned my radio up!' I lie. Wine was my volume; it worked and I didn't care.

'We've never heard that!' he says, glaring—redirecting his boiling blood that's been aimed at her for the past few hours, now pointed at me instead. Knowing little of me, other than the nothing-man assumptions. Only I know whether it's a good idea for him to push too hard at me or not, if at all. Even the over-preened idiot starts to see something behind my facade now as I stare back with the black of my eyes.

'Well, I use headphones; I don't like to intrude on a neighbour's space.' My words are softly spoken but my eyes are the windows to a world he's never been, and wouldn't ever want to—he can see it.

His eyes diffuse and dissolve any misplaced verbal attack he may have had ideas about, and they both grin, looking at each other, and walk slowly on, leaving me feeling that I've somehow pushed them past their own quarrels by becoming a common enemy. In half an hour's time I imagine they alternate tongues down each other's throats with brief verbal digs and smears over their sad neighbour downstairs—the nothing man—an easy target.

'Night!' he says over his shoulder, holding her tightly, his prize. His ego glows up the staircase at me; I'd like to snap it in two and send it shattering to the ground floor in pieces, but I don't.

'Nice night!' she says, turning slightly and throwing me enough of a glance to cloud my train of thought, which was mainly on avoiding engaging with them. Too late: she was now in my head, with her deep cherry hair. The only female interaction or glimmer of affection I've had since being placed under protection.

He tenses his grip on her shoulder, fingers whitening as he steers her away, moving her on before I can get a glimpse at those tear-soaked green Irish eyes again. I refocus and let them both walk further on down the stairs.

I imagine briefly as I stand alone in the staircase that the next time they argue it's worse: he leaves, and she comes down to seek comfort with her deep red hair, tight body and green eyes. A flit, a fantasy, a blink of an imagined better life experience and then it's gone.

I listen for the door downstairs to close before I continue down two flights, passing by the piles of mail for past and present residents, and some possibly for me. The mail in the corridor looks like a daily evolving mass of unclaimed mysterious envelopes, unopened greetings cards and bills. If there is ever anything that catches my interest when searching for my own mail, and I think it's for a past resident or sometimes even a current one, I take it upstairs and open it as a lucky dip to see what's inside. Mainly this is without success, but sometimes there'll be a lost sincerity from a distant relative, a free gift from the Reader's Digest or a membership letter for an obscure club. A few seconds of entertainment for me, and an empathy test putting myself in other people's skin, heads and lives for a while.

My identity hasn't been my own since the protection started and maybe long before that, when it belonged to another authority. I'm getting used to the madness and the boredom. The reinventions I give myself with a second or two in other people's mail often turns out to be good therapy, and training for something in my new identity I haven't thought up and moved onto yet.

I continue out into the rain, turn left going up the hill and head to my nearest and the first pub I've been to since being here, in this city of Bristol. I walk up to the bar which is by now three to four people (students) deep all trying to get served. The Aussie barman, who has by now begun to recognise my patterns, raises his eyebrows at me and mouths a silent greeting—fuck off—smiling and returning to his busy taps.

'Alright?' he says, when I'm halfway through the mass at the bar.

'Yes,' I say, and glance at the beer tap between me, him and the thirsty students. They don't know what real thirst is yet. It's a party time vocation for them, a loan syphon and an extension of raiding mum's drinks cabinet whilst she's out for the night— they just don't know it yet.

The barman nods reassuringly and does nothing for me through the crowd, but when I get to the front line I'm served straight away. The four or five part-time drinkers that have been there a while shrug in disapproval. A weak and harmless response.

The pub is seemingly all students as I look around and I feel awkward, but I'd be awkward anywhere anyhow, so stay. I'm into my fourth lager before I gain any confidence in my surroundings. These people ooze arrogance and optimism in their futures whilst I'm a blank slate—not even the drinks stick to it; I'm paper thin.

The 9pm surge subsides and I'm perched against one of the serving areas, scribbling in my Moleskine notebook when another loner attempts a conversation with me.

'Hi, what are you on?'

I mention something non-descript, then, 'Stella.'

'What?'

'Grolsch.' I change beer, same message.

'What course?' he re-questions.

'Haloperidol,' I say, moving away from him along the bar.

He must have a basic knowledge of antipsychotics as he looks apprehensive and then moves away too.

I'm not on the drugs myself, but I know them as fellow ex-service members were given them liberally for PTSD, bipolar and depression after all we'd seen and been through. Maybe I should be on something like that, but I can't imagine admitting a weakness for now, and continue instead to drown it all out in drink. At some point this might prove to be the cause rather than cure, but for now though I have a thirst, I feed off it, and the pub is my surrogate mother, the taps dripping life into me like teats.

I feel it's getting time to go on to a club. The bar is filling again as it nears closing time, and my head is starting to drift off as mother's teats do their work. I feel subdued by memories I can't talk about anymore, and by any responsibility I might find in the vocation I've been handed. I walk out and into the rain again; it washes away some of the sweat and oiliness from the beer and bar. I run my hands across my face and into my hair, feeling better—better than bad.

I meander vaguely on a downhill route to where I had intended earlier, but hadn't had the drive to go. I daydream my way by the waterfront, close enough to see and hear the drunken antics from the riverside bars. Girls are running, shoes in hand, black skirts riding high, one strap off a shoulder and screeching like tortured animals. The men shove one another, a soup of pastel Ben Sherman shirts brawling, talking to mates over shoulders whilst pissing up against windows, walls, into shadows and each other.

I keep a safe and weary distance from the scum of over-friendly drunks that would inevitably be skimmed off by club closing time. Not too close to get caught up in it, I find my space and enjoy it, as I'm not ready for that. I'm daydreaming, walking alone. A target for some maybe, but they can all smell it too: the pointless and fruitless interaction. Worse, if they were to look a little closer and ask for the time, my wallet or change, they'd see they'd lose teeth, break an arm or end up in the docks. It's in the eyes and you can't make it go away. A false name won't cover up a history in the eyes, bones and blood; muscle memories that won't forget.

The club queue I get to is painless; it's almost without a wait and then I'm up the boarding ramp and down into the bowels of a boat in the docks. I think I love the music, as I hear a familiar Manchester bassline and drums that echo through the corridors, the stairs, around the boat below, my head and my memories. I pay and look with anticipation towards the way in and a girl takes my cash and stamps my hand with a smudged four-leaf clover.

I walk to the bar downstairs in the largest room, which has a stage where the hold once was. I order a cider and a shot of tequila to keep it company and stay for another two rounds, assessing characters that come and go. Some are staggering but articulate with their orders. Some are very slow, steady and over-considered in their approach but stammer undecipherable nonsense: stoned. I wonder what I'm like from the outside, sober a little, don't like it, so stop thinking and follow the smell.

A tasty stench of a strong, skunk-like weed fills the air, wafting over from the DJ booth to the left of the long bar. The only filter is a pair of black curtains, stained from so many nights of spills, thrills and smokes. I think they used to be white. The curtain moves back and forth as the huge black security guards stick their heads in and out of the booth. I know that routine in any city, Bristol's no different. Their authoritative glances and stares mask the real reasons for the DJ's need for over-the-top protection as he deals out as many cellophane envelopes as tunes. For a moment I wish I was a big black security guard. After another two rounds of tequilas and ciders, in my head I am a big black security guard, and I find myself sharing a smoke with the DJ and his pals looking out to the shadows writhing out of time on the dance floor.

I alternate between the DJ booth, pissing and standing near a mass lacking co-ordination on the dance floor, and head to the bar to keep topping myself up when needed. Later I start to feel full and walk to the front and lean against the stage next to a short dark-haired pixie-looking girl, who might be my type—I can't remember. The smoke, strobes and darkness filter any senses, as does the cider and tequila mix.

She has a fat friend and duffle-coat-wearing tall man with her who definitely aren't my type; drinks, memory failures or not. The fat girl says something which I half-hear and half-ignore. The man then starts saying something, stoops, and then is yelling in my ear. I nod to avoid conflict and show some attention, which is really elsewhere, thinking about the pixie-looking girl.

My mind is mainly with his short dark-haired friend as I roll and light a cigarette from the contents of my coat pocket. I feel a head rush and sickness building soon after. The short dark-haired girl comes across and starts talking and suddenly everything else is just white noise in my way, and I become aware of a feeling of sickness that's a real bitter soundtrack to the attempted chat-up.

'Are you here on your own?' she asks.

'I've just moved here for work. I don't know many people yet, other than work people. I just thought I'd get out and see who I might meet,' I shout.

'What?' she says.

'Yes, I'm on my own.'

I take another drag on the cigarette, both arms leaning on the stage, trying to look good whilst feeling even sicker with each passing second, turning green if the lights were up to see.

'That's cool,' she says, 'coming out on your own, having a good time. I would never think of doing that. I'd end up staying in, getting drunk on my own before I'd do that!'

'I do that too,' I say. 'That was breakfast!'

'What do you do?'

'Design, I think.'

'Brilliant! My friend really likes Jim Morrison. Would you do a painting on her bedroom wall? She'd be really made up.'

I stop listening, and start imagining fucking her and it pollutes the conversation.

'Would you? Would you? Painting?'

'How old are you?' I ask.

'Eighteen…You can paint can't you? We've tried loads of times but it comes out wrong.'

'Are you still at school?'

'No, I work at AXA as a secretary,' she says.

'Where do you live, nearby? I live just twenty minutes away.'

'What?'

'Do you fuck?' I finish, and leave to be sick.

No Future. That's what the graffiti on the building opposite my flat says in blood-red childish scribbles. I know now it's right, a change is needed. I'm Nothing Man.

2

I wake up alone remembering the girl's name from the night before: Gemma. And where she works: AXA, as a secretary. If I remember that much over the next week, I tell myself I'll try and reach out to her at work, try and be normal, interact, attempt a relationship or something real people like that do.

Wandering through my flat in a haze, I look with contempt at the scribbles in my notebook from the night before and turn it face down. The empty wine bottles that litter the table lie around, notes and papers all painting a picture of a lost mind, my lost mind and identity. My head throbs at the sight of the empty bottles and it's enough to make me want a drink or to throw up; I'm undecided so I put on some clothes and leave my flat to go outside and decide out there whilst I fill my lungs with the city's dirty air.

I start to walk my hangover off between record shops and coffee houses. They're all overrun with couples, arm in arm, whispering, smiling and beaming with contentment after extended Sunday-morning sex sessions before God. I've always thought Saturday is a great day to be single and Sunday just isn't.

A seagull shits on me and I return to the bar that started me towards the hangover in the first place, for a hair of the dog. A famous yellow cartoon family is on a big screen in the corner and I feign awkward interest, to look less like I'm just there to drink and lean against the bar. It reaches early evening and the bar soon fills with another glut of students searching for hangover cures as well—mainly cider, which is the south-west's cure and the cursed spray of many a toilet cubical after seven pints on an empty stomach.

The barmaid catches me looking at her chest after my second drink and I decide to have a third and see if it will make me brave enough to look at her straight in the face. When I do look it's too late, and the staff have changed shift. The replacement barmaid is rough and I'll need at least another three drinks before I can look at her for any time longer than I've tried already.

I catch sight of my reflection in a mirror behind the bar. I would run out in shame at how I look had I not topped up the alcohol levels from the night before, and anyway, I'm between personalities in which to care about such things yet. I look like I've walked through the rain to get there and it's a clear sky outside; my wetness is beer sweat and a shed load of the day-after-the-night-before self-loathing.

The yellow cartoon family is into its third round and I'm now genuinely interested. I've forgotten how many drinks I've had and I'm also genuinely interested in the once considered rough barmaid too. It's now my reason, an excuse to drink past curing a hangover and to stay there drinking myself drunk again.

The barman announces over the music that it's 'tequila night' and I wonder if I'm going to make it into work tomorrow, my first day at the new place. 'Tequila night' was when the barman would pour a tequila and you'd give him a pound, he'd toss the coin, and you'd call it; if you won, the tequila was yours and he'd poor another tequila, toss the coin again and you'd call it again, and so on. And so it did go on, and shortly I was into my seventh, having only paid for three.

My hair of the dog had grown a big body, and before I started work tomorrow it would form teeth and bite me straight through to the bone again.

3

The therapist assigned to me with the witness protection had told me to be creative: draw, write and paint—whatever, to get by and externalise my feelings. All without expressing anything that might expose my past—but what else would be grinding away at me inside but my past, and an attempt at a future? The little white notebook she'd given me had it all, spilled out on the pages and growing day by day, and if it stopped evolving, so would I.

Going to an office of repressed zombies really doesn't help the metamorphosis process. They all need a little white notebook there, or ten, the ones that can be saved anyway. The rest can drop through the floor for all I care; soulless, robotic office lizards the lot of them.

In the morning, I put on the only ill-fitting suit that was given to me, and wander to work, each step filled with resentment. This isn't me, not without a rifle in my hand. I agree with myself to just get through it all—work that is—and survive the week. Don't piss anyone off—do what little you can get away with and live for the weekend, evenings and drink.

I pass through the security guards like I'm a ghost and they don't even look up from their desk, then go around the circular lobby to an even bigger circular donut of a building complete with an atrium in the centre that looks out of bounds other than to ducks and seagulls. The guard takes my name and tells me to go to the top floor, phase two, then to suck off the first person to ask who I am and why I'm there. At least, that's how it replays in my head as I head up the stairs to my new corporate safe house. I'm bored already, and haven't even sat at a desk yet. Doomed to mainstream society's paper-pushing oblivion.

I'm intercepted and walked around the office to be introduced to the department. The guy introducing me is just about as lacking in enthusiasm after seven years there as I am after a few minutes—he has my sympathy and contempt all at once.

'This is John, he's our new designer,' he says.

'John Barrie,' I say, and so it goes on like that, round and round. No one gives a fuck, least of all me, and after twenty-something introductions I feel a hungover nausea kicking in and need to drink, or eat, shit or all three. We only make it a fraction round the office in pods of desks and I decide to distract myself by trying to make wisecracks to liven it up a bit whilst holding my bowels in place.

'This is John Barrie,' he says to a short fat old woman, who has a tight perm and the essence of something attractive turned bad. She giggles irrelevantly at a joke that no one's made or is ever going to make. She laughs just to get by I guess, and get through the day—it's her mechanism for dealing with this life she's in; everyone's got a self-distraction trick.

'John, this is Karen, she's a technician, she's been here for years and anything you want help with she'll be great.'

She giggles to herself again. 'I'm Karen and I'm here for technical support.'

'And to laugh inanely, like a *Carry On* film character too it seems…' I add, loud enough to be heard, whilst quiet enough to not be understood. Blunt, cold and cruel, I feel immediately bad, but maybe it'll turn out to have been cruel to be kind if I can snap her out of this little routine of polite giggles at nothing, if only for a moment. That broken record she's in stuck on the spot, a skipping record in time, will only get worse as she's clearly going nowhere. The giggles getting more and more forced, intense and manic each time until she eventually can't take it anymore and breaks down, throwing a tie-wearing idiot from the balcony for asking to borrow her stapler or the precious hole punch she's nicknamed Reg.

I think whoever it would be would probably deserve to go flying, as sexism has obviously flooded this place for decades. The fact she's nearing retirement and is a technician and I've seen suit-wearing boys young enough to be her children strutting the corridors and walkways like managers is all sickening.

She stops laughing abruptly and I'm moved on to the next person who seems to be a very proper-speaking middle-aged man in a bad tank top and Farah slacks. I whisper 'gay sailor' under my breath and don't take any notice of the dialogue around me. Later I whisper 'anal fool' to another random corporate sort. It's risky but it's all that stops me vomiting or shitting my pants at people and it kills some time before lunch and a drink.

It takes me twenty minutes to walk home in my lunch break, bypassing the pubs and bars on the waterfront like a minefield of distractions. I try to sleep a bit of my hangover off, rather than drinking it off for a change; I've only got twenty minutes or so. I walk back and stop for a pint and a short on the way instead. My boss—an old grey fat man with the presence of a TV granddad, complete with the disappointed look over the top of rimmed glasses—realises my condition and gives me a variety of mundane skill-free tasks to do. I don't mind; I don't want to think, I just want rest then another drink before this whole bore-circus of a dog machine starts over again.

I'm on the ground floor near the entrance, far away from my

colleagues in an adjoining building more the shape of a banana than the other, which is donut-shaped. I'm photocopying the pile the boss gave me of what feels like hundreds of documents, all of which would be the same if it wasn't for some very minor variations. I wonder if this task and these documents are designed for punishing new employees with hangovers, and how many trees have been wasted on the exercise in the past.

The task is boring enough to induce sleep but different enough to require occasional attention. I suspect the job has in fact been handed down through the years. The grey, old, fat man probably already copied all of these by hand forty years before me. A thankless task born out of some superiors sheer bloody mindedness before the invention of the photocopier—when he was caught having a snifter at lunch—the bastard.

A cute brunette starts to use the copy machine next to me, and I feel better about it all. I glance at her out of the corner of my eye and she is stunning. She moves like she doesn't notice the eyes all around checking her out. If she did notice, maybe she'd lift her head, sway her hips more and maybe even wear tighter clothes.

She's in unconventional office clothes. I wonder if she's a student temping to pay her course fees, or just a creative caught out of context, suppressed between one corporate milling machine and another.

I finish the documents and give myself more of them to do in order to spend more time near to where she works. I don't see her again and the impatience makes the remaining time fly by.

The day finishes just as the drink haze has lifted and just as I get interested in something: her.

4

I've reached Thursday, and my fourth hangover of the week. The people in the office have learned my name, even if I haven't theirs. I've been there four days and already someone is leaving. I've been invited to the drinks after work and I expect a free drink or two.

I go along to the pub at the bottom of the hill that is Park Street, mainly thinking of the amount of rounds of drinks I can jump between without buying one, rather than being sociable.

I'm on the verge of nausea by the time I reach the bar, with a restless anxiety that needs a sip of something toxic to calm it back down. They've all been drinking for an hour or so by the time I arrive and the otherwise anally retentive sorts ride the alcohol-driven waves of tit jokes. They sneer at strangers who hover in the background, minding their own business. The people from my work are in a far corner, some in the shadows leering out, as women and others sit gossiping around tables and start to exchange secrets and insipid office politics. One of the girls from the office is at the bar getting a round in.

'Hey it's John, John-boy Barrie, everybody!' she says, as I lean alongside her against the bar.

'What do you want? I've just got them in,' she asks.

'Stella, I think.'

'And a Stella please, barman, as well!' The barman pours the drink and slides it at her together with the other drinks she's ordered.

'That'll be another two twenty for his,' he says.

She pays and pushes the pint through a soup of ash and spillage, further down the bar towards me.

'I suppose for that you'll want two-twenty's worth of conversation?' I remark blankly, looking over the rim of the glass and taking a sip.

She glares at me for a while and I smile back wryly and take another mouthful. She then raises her knee sharply into my groin and starts screaming like a banshee. People lunge and grab at her from the shadows and hold her back as she writhes around, determined to get another kick in. She screeches at me and I try to save as much beer in the glass as I can while stumbling back and forth, then I walk off to find a corner to hide in with my balls ringing.

Later I find myself at the secrets table. The people exchange office gossip and shamelessly stroke each other's point of view which is nothing more than idle bullshit. The woman who kicked me in the groin features quite highly in the varying topics and it seems to me most of them have or want to fuck her but won't say it out loud, so instead badmouth her like they're kids in a playground. I realise fast that she's infinitely more interesting than these gossiping morons, if she's done half of what they're talking about. I have nothing to contribute and so sit in silence getting progressively more drunk.

Fortunately, my bouncing between rounds works—my wallet remains full. At some point I ask why they don't just spit on her back, like the horny disgruntled teenagers they are, if they fancy a ride. They're too wrapped up in themselves to hear, understand or care. They're five, ten and some of them twenty-plus years programmed into this office mechanic. Resistance is futile; it must be something in the vending-machine coffee they drink.

Two more free drinks and I change which group to sit with, and which round to hijack. I join a group of four who don't want to be there, in that bar, or so they moan. Not only do they not want to be there, but they don't want to be in the company. Honest sorts, at least. They all sound as though they believe they are meant for better things. It's comforting, even with all of their mouthing off and pretensions.

As a newcomer I'm reluctant to join in, as years in service seems to be commonplace as a theme for bitching. The longer you've been with the company the longer it seems you can have the floor, stand on the soap box to moan, and with a heightened vigour and approval from the rest of the table. These people drink the most: a pint every twenty minutes. They also seem to hate everyone there, themselves most. I like these people more and more; they have perspective—blaming everyone and everything for their own demise, finishing with a frustration at their ugly selves for selling out in the first place. Damn the draw of the pound and need to integrate in society. In another parallel universe they'd be painters, goat farmers, make cider and their own cheese, or so it goes on.

'If only the day job didn't suck so much life out of them, they would go on… escape the bitterness—they might make it—have a life with value, rather than be another cog in the engine or a dog in the machine.' I think. The words feeling like a third party on my shoulder passing judgment, taunting and whispering an ominous fate at me like a baby sledgehammer against an already fractured pane, poised, ready to shatter.

And so it does—It shatters apart.

Most things do, before giving rise to something else. We're all just made up from the star dust of the original break-up of the pieces.

I find myself drunk and by the bar talking to a middle-aged

woman who has a rough, north-western accent. She is clearly broken by the system, and probably the lowest paid person in relation to their age in here, more due to her IQ than the sexist policy of a late 90s corporate hole she's in.

She pretends to listen to a variety of things I'm saying just in order to wait her turn to speak, all of it pure shit. I try not to, but I hate her and am getting bored to my bones as she's literally talking me into a trance.

'Yes really, it's unbelievable,' she says after a few sentences have just fallen out of us both and passed me by without a sense of point or any true meaning at all. 'I just don't believe it, she's like on the edge—totally. I mean, how come she doesn't get fired or something?' she continues.

'I think she must pay her way in ways more recognisable to her superiors,' I say and wink. Unnoticed.

'Yes, yes she is a liability. One day she will, just like... you know... get at the wrong one!' She goes on and I realise she's talking about the girl who'd corrected my ball arrangement earlier.

'I don't care—why should you?' I ask.

'It's just like, I don't know, like she doesn't care. I could do her job for half the money and be ten times as grateful. Don't you think?' she asks, again ignoring my words.

'No.'

'Exactly, I mean, what do you do? It must be more than her and for what?' she asks, drawing it all out painfully further; on and on she goes. I give up and cut it dead:

'I fuck dogs—I'm a dog fucker!' I move my hips with hands holding something invisible about the size of a large greyhound. My words stop her dead—mission accomplished—and she can't speak anymore. Thank the god of bad manners and contrition.

She looks like I've thrown an ice bucket over her head,

mutters something uninteresting and gags a little, then leaves for the toilet. I've been relieved mentally and now want to leave physically, so I wave, smile and tip a non-existent hat to the woman who'd given me a knee to my gonads, then go out into the night.

5

Friday drags on and means nothing to me. I try to make contact with the girl I'd met in the club on a boat. All I have to trace her is her first name, what she does and for who. I decide to call the switch board of AXA and ask to speak to Gemma. I've no doubt they've thousands of people there, but what else have I got to do this afternoon? And the weekend is coming. Without anything to stop me going mad, I need something or someone to aim for, a project, person, task to believe in.

'Do you know how many people we have working here?' a female voice barks from the reception line.

'No, and please try—it is important. She's expecting my call,' I press politely, my tone suggesting there might be more to the call, more than just a drunken encounter from a few nights ago that is.

'There's two thousand plus, at least,' she affirms.

'Gemma. Please?' I press.

I could hear her talking and mocking with her workmate nearby with the words just hang up and idiot both used in a much thicker Bristolian accent than their telephone voices.

'Gemma please, she's a secretary there!'

'Oh Gemma—I'll try Jan. Jan, yes, I'll do that. I think she might work with a Gemma, I'll put you through,' she says, and her tone switches from irritated suspicion to relief at being given a way of getting rid of me politely other than the obvious hang-up.

Anticipating being passed around without a result, I get ready to hang up myself.

'Hello, this is Jan's phone, Gemma Layon speaking. How can I help?'

'Hi, Gemma Layon. Its John, John Barrie, from Saturday night.'

'Who?'

'John, from that club on the boat—you wanted a picture of Jim Morrison and all that stuff,' I say, my confidence waning a little at the *who?* comment; obviously my vague essence of a new personality was no more apparent or impressionable to others than it was myself.

After a disjointed reintroduction, I entice her into meeting me for lunch and some drinks. We meet by the waterfront in a bar that serves as much coffee as lager. I turn up early and order a beer with a chaser, which is turning into a really bad, splintered crutch to lean on—but I like it, and it's good to like something as simple as a drink when it feels like you are, and have, nothing. One or two and you can feel rejuvenated—a someone charging into life's next battle. Or it's just liquid armour for another awkward conversation, a lubricant to an uneasy attempted courtship, like now.

Anyway, I can't stop drinking; it is, and always will be in my blood.

She's late, looks scared, nervous and young as she walks in— it's all good. It's been drizzling outside and her hair's matted to her head—it's really good. We've nothing in common to talk about so I drink and she does the same, without encouragement. Between awkward small talk I finish my fourth beer and realise it's mid-afternoon and I'm too late to go back to work without unwanted attention from the rest of them in the corporate milling machine.

It turns out Gemma doesn't work Friday afternoons and I'm jealous so I claim the same to her, like it's something we might share in common, but then I go to find a phone outside to call in sick. I glance at her through the window, half-checking she's still there and half-checking she still looks good, whilst an obvious escape route is still open to me. She still looks nervous; drunk now, but still cute. I manage to explain to the office secretary over the payphone about a sudden stomach upset, meaning I don't think I'll be returning to work.

'The shits'—no one pushes too hard to query the shits… She sounds unconvinced and curt though, shits or not. I had avoided the noise from the bar speakers by going outside, although I could have used the phone in there, but I hadn't foreseen a passing homeless person kicking his dog and calling it a cunt. I decide to hang up and then call him the same, before feeling bad, then give him all the change in my pocket. Times are hard—worse for him; them all. It feels bad.

I return to Gemma inside. She's there hunched up in her big coat in the corner. We drink and try to find a connection rather than me just wanting to sleep with her, or thinking it might do me good to integrate back into real life, date, fuck and get on with it like everyone else. Every time I go to the toilet, which grows in frequency, I expect her not to be there when I get back, but there she always is, scared and cute on my return, looking ready to flee but never doing it.

Whenever she goes to the toilet I try to finish my drink and have an extra round waiting. I manage to get a few more pints of lager into the small girl and then suggest going back to my flat for a smoke. She surprisingly accepts.

I lie about how close I live to the bar, saying it's just ten minutes away. Every ten minutes we walk, she asks about my flat and what's in it and how far away it is again. The rain gets heavier. It was lighter earlier; it had less guilt to wash off then. Later, I feel sure it will pour down over me and wash it all away.

I sit on my armchair; she's on the far end of the settee. We have two joints and I start rolling a third.

'How come you've no TV, and hardly any furniture?' she asks.

'I've just moved here, I haven't set up camp yet.'

'You could be a psycho or anything. I shouldn't have come.'

'But we're having such fun,' I lie. My heart's not in it and I'm not a rapist in any identity past or present—so the lack of intention or slowed interest must be about as attractive to her as the home-brand economy supermarket condoms sitting on the bedside table.

My head swims more and more and, by the end of the third smoke, I'm getting hard with the weed even if my head isn't committed. I excuse myself to the toilet, quietly stand and walk past her to the next room. She doesn't shift her gaze from the window and the lights of the city outside.

Looking at myself in the mirror whilst running the cold tap, I splash water on my face, take a piss and reach for my wash bag from the top of the bathroom cabinet. There's a surgeon's scalpel I keep in the inside pocket. I take it out, sit on the toilet cistern with my feet on the lid and run the blade lightly across the veins on the back of my hand.

As I press the blade to my veins that are itching and bulging with the pollution inside, I think of a time when I was with an old friend in a beer garden in Manchester. He was big, offensive and always overly aggressive for no other reason than it was his way. It got him what he wanted most of the time, even if other times it resulted in a smack or punch to the head for him. As we sat there in the north-west's attempt at sunshine, a fly buzzed in front of his face and he swore at it. The fly then walked around the rim of his beer and he waved at it. It came to rest just underneath his raised hand and I can remember how sure I was he was going to just kill it, but he just brushed it to one side instead and it recovered and flew away. When I asked why he didn't just kill it he said it wasn't a challenge, it was pointless—and those few seconds stayed with me.

When I return through to the sitting room Gemma is standing up waiting to use the bathroom and I assume leave shortly after. The city lights flash outside, casting an orange disco onto her face. She walks straight past me. I stay in the corridor and when she returns and tries to squeeze past me, I ask to hold her.

'What?!' she responds.

I take hold of her, squeeze her, her arms by her side, and I feel really good; the weed has heightened my sense of well-being and touch. The slightest physical contact drives me into a quilted dream. When I take my arms away she's glaring and a tear runs down her face and drops from her chin onto my foot. I'm much harder now.

'I'm going to go,' she murmurs.

She grabs her coat and walks fast, out of the flat. I try to find words to get her to stay but she's listening less than earlier in the day which wasn't much. I hear her irregular footsteps stumbling down the staircase outside. I sit back down, pick up a half-finished joint from the ashtray, try to smile and inhale it deep down into my lungs.

'Game over,' I say, thinking, *I can't do real life, not yet.*

The footsteps return, rushing in a panic, and I stand up with head spinning and wander over to open the front door before a knock can come. I open the door to see Gemma there. She's crying a lot now, arm raised pre-knock to the door.

'I forgot my bag,' she gurgles through tears, then rushes past me, grabs the bag and runs out.

'You're weird—a psycho,' she says over her shoulder.

'You're too young,' I say back; I hadn't done anything. She was too young. She also started off very pretty, which was misleading as she quickly lost those looks after a few pints and some weed—despite the involuntary erection. Most women are exactly the opposite, and get better the more you consume. That's her bad luck I guess—but I'm not like everybody else. I don't feel bad, I have no need.

Outside though, the rain has still decided to pour as I'd thought it might earlier—the sky has opened up to wash away all that I have in me; the sins of my subconscious, my past and present.

6

'All surface, no feeling. It's just the way it is,' I say to the room. I eventually stop throwing away drunken comments to the black guy next to me. He has two watches on each wrist, and trainers encrusted with a layering of blackness from wandering the streets. I move on and leave him to his madness, alone—there's no hope for company in either of us with my idle attempt at an exchange.

I recognise the girl from near the photocopier at work; she's at the far end of a bar I've chosen to drink my Saturday away in, talking at a mad man who doesn't listen. She looks stunning and is with another girl equally as stunning, but not my thing.

After a while I'm drunk and overconfident enough to invite myself to sit with them. With my past identity buried and without any new ID to speak of, I steal my confidence from a number of characters I know from life and on-screen who aren't me, unless I need them like here and now, to talk to a pretty girl in a bar.

After a few beers, these borrowed personalities are all mine; they're the me I need for now and more; it's all an act I'm putting on to deceive me as much as the girls. It works and I act out another person's set routine and steal their applause, reminding me of a trick my mother once taught me at school when I was terrified to jump in the deep end of the swimming pool.

I couldn't swim at the time and the swimming teacher was like an angry old military bear bobbing around in there snarling and ordering us all to swallow our fears and to just jump in at him. Three things scared me: the bear of a man snarling at me, the deep blue water and drowning. The more we hesitated, the angrier he got, and the more fearful we got. He was as scary as the deep waters, but together they made for something terrifying to a young boy.

My mother's advice was simple and I've used it since to face many a bear or deep water, of a kind. She said, 'If you're scared, pretend to be someone else you know who wouldn't be. Pick a strong character and just get on with it.' It worked, and I've been displacing my fears in situations where I know I need strength onto any number of unsuspecting actors, friends and family members as I pretend to be them to get by and be normal—whatever that is. The words, 'You're strong, I know you can do it!' never left her mouth, but instead words accepting she knew I was weak—as did I—and that I needed to be someone else in life to achieve anything.

As I got older I realised her sentiment might have meant more. Maybe the realisation hit me that everyone has barriers and to break through them we need a mechanism—our knowledge of this is what makes us strong; whoever and whatever we use to just get on with it, get the job done. When I eventually jumped in the pool, something worse than the bear waited for me, or the deep waters, or drowning... I hadn't tied my trunks tight enough. They rose to the top without me and when I broke the surface, the girls at the poolside were bent over the tiled floor, pointing and spitting with laughter, destroying what little a boy of that age had—and it was very little.

The more I talk to the girls in the bar, the happier I feel, and the more the one that I prefer listens, the more I want her. I flirt with cynicisms about our corporate trap of an employer and she joins in. I find out her friend is actually her sister, she hates where she works, she likes me, and I feel like a beer-soaked god, for a while. We leave and drunkenly exchange phone numbers outside in the rain. I don't ask for her sister's number. She's not my thing.

All surface no feeling.

7

I sleep heavy, dreaming of escaping from a prison in the centre of an endless desert. I get out past the security guards with my only treasured possession, a goldfish. I scale high walls, jump between rooftops and drop down into the sand over and over to get out of the endless complex I'm trapped in. All this is done whilst avoiding detection, and with my goldfish slopping about in its bowl. I hardly spill a drop from its life source—the water. I hang and drop from the last perimeter wall into baking sands below. My bare feet burn in the sands and I look down at my fish, in its bowl, and then rest it on the sand to let the water settle. The water finally stops sloshing from side to side and becomes calm again. My fish, which I've taken with me on this escape over rooftops and walls without spilling a drop of its water, jumps from its bowl and lies in the sand to fry and I look on, letting it burn. I wake up the moment the fish, in the dream, has finished scorching a silhouette into the hard sand.

Leaving my flat that morning, down the stairs and into the hallway I pass another pile of unclaimed mail. My eyes are drawn to a brown envelope amongst the sea of white bills and flyers which has a scrawled name on it. It might be for me, I don't know—another lucky dip. I pocket it and save it for later.

Work drags hazily on, beer sweat stinging my eyes.

'I had a dream I escaped from a desert prison last night, with a goldfish, and then it killed itself by jumping out of the bowl and fried itself on the hot sand!' I say to the guy on the desk next to me. 'I enjoyed it, it was strange, and don't know what it means—not sure I want to either.'

'I know what it means,' he says and grins.

Within a few days of me working here this same colleague had announced his unashamed born-again Christian credentials, and preached at my empty ears and soul.

'You struggle your way through your shallow, faithless, drunken life. Your faith is as imprisoned as you are, my friend!'

'Really?' I nod, glaring sarcastically.

'In the end,' he continues, 'you'll think you've got somewhere to be, but for you and your faith it'll be too late! A fish frying in the sand as your futile faithless life.'

'That's fascinating,' I nod again. 'Want a coffee?' And I stand up and go to the machine that's in a room at the end of the office. While I'm there I pour a little of his drink out into the recycling, undo my fly and top his cup up with a dose of my warm, drunken, faithless piss.

'You think it's really too late for me?' I say handing him his penance.

'No no, Jesus is always reaching out.'

That night I bump into the unconventional girl from near the copier at work and her sister and before leaving for a club, her boyfriend joins us. I check out her sister again to see if I can claim something back from the night, but she's still not my thing. I finish my drink and continue to check out copier girl: Lisa.

'He's always upsetting me, he's mean.' Lisa leans into me, flirting with the suggestion of a possibility of something between us. I get the impression she loves the three sets of eyes on her. One set protective from her boyfriend, another set the envious eyes of her sister at the attention she's getting from both us men. And then there are those from me, stirring the whole situation up a bit. How long this sisterly rivalry has gone on in their twenty-five years drawing air I don't know. Drinking on and on I get bitter and look forward to a conclusion, preferably in the form of a freak accident pushing her and him apart, and her into me.

We get to a club on All Saints Street with a German name. Talk is sparse and the air is thick with competition as we stick to the beer-soaked carpet. We dance badly, me and Lisa more in sync, the others not. When her boyfriend goes to the toilet, her sister makes herself scarce by going to the bar, and Lisa and I dance cradling each other. She shouts how he mistreats her and I go to feel more of her, nodding reassuringly.

'He never has time for me. Just football, and the pub!' she yells.

'That's awful,' I tell her, holding her close, listening all the more intently, one hand (left) resting on her arse and the other (right) on her chest.

He returns after we've finished looking into each other's eyes and separated from our hold. He picks up on a small leftover something between us, an understanding, the chemistry, and he glares into the mass of shadows from people dancing behind us and then goes to the bar alone.

'Yes, he's so mean,' I say, shake my head and smile, thinking of her naked. I look on to where he's gone to the bar and my mind wanders, imagining him gagged and bound under the bed where we might come together for the first time.

The club has a dark, smoky and gothic feel to it, the music a mix of white-noise industrial guitar cut into timeless dance tunes, and the people are a mix of leather-clad, pierced, troubled teens, baggy indie kids and us. I look forward to any songs that involve mindless jumping around so I can jump into Lisa. Or better—jump between her and her boyfriend.

It all ends and we get a blue cab back. Me, Lisa, her sister, her boyfriend and an elephant in the room all crushed into the back of a five-seater. The elephant in the room and I take the flip-down seats behind the driver's cab.

'Where do you want dropping?' the cabby asks.

'Shall we go back to mine? Ours?' Lisa says then corrects herself. 'Fancy some dark rum and spliff? He's just brought some back from holiday,' she asks, looking at me with one hand on her boyfriend.

'That'd be a laugh,' her sister says coldly, sarcastically, looking out of the window.

'Why not,' I say, looking back at my sweating palms. Where's the harm in a drink and smoke between warring factions? I think. A pipe of peace. Is this a pre-war ceremony? I think on.

I can see dandruff, redness and flaking in the back of the cabby's head as we pull up to the road which Lisa's place is on. The reflection of the cabby's eyes in the mirror shows black holes without feeling. He twitches awkwardly, half growls and clears his throat. Reaching into my pocket to check for change, I happen across the brown envelope I'd picked up from my hallway earlier. I open a corner and run a finger inside.

'What's that?' Lisa's sister asks, distracted from her daydreaming out of the window by the tearing noise.

The taxi halts suddenly and the taxi driver stares ahead, twitches three times, flakes floating down from his head before he turns to us.

'Fare—six pounds, six, fare, six pounds!' he yells into the back.

We jump, apart from Lisa's boyfriend who stops glaring at me and glares at the taxi driver instead. I return the opened envelope to my pocket, whilst thinking that if I hadn't pissed into one of his disciples' coffees, maybe God would bring this taxi driver and Lisa's mistake for a man together and distract him for a while, while I take care of matters with his girl—it doesn't happen though.

Lisa's flat is small, with low ceilings and woodchip on the walls. The place for woodchip isn't here in this cute girl's flat, it's in trees. She pours four glasses of rum as her man rolls a joint. Her sister downs her drink and excuses herself to leave just the three of us. Two of us wanting a drink, a joint and then sex, the other wanting a drink, a joint, to rip my head off and then sex. The rum is sweet and the joint is heavy as we sit in silence in the sitting room, all on separate seats. I grin inanely and occasionally lift the ashtray to catch some ash, never returning it to the same place, so when I need it again I have to have a little nervous pretend look for it each time.

'I'm going to bed,' he announces. 'What are you doing?' asking all around.

'Now?' she asks, playfully.

'Now,' he says to her then turns to me. 'And you, you don't live miles away do you!' he states as a matter of fact.

'But you can rest up here for a bit if you're too caned on that settee—we've had lots of friends sleep there, it's okay,' she finishes for him, before he can verbally throw me out and shut the door on me.

I don't respond, but just slowly close my eyes, put my feet up and my head down and smile. I hear mumbling and occasional raised voices as they disappear into the other room. 'Friend?' and then, 'Really… friends?' are mentioned a few times before a door is shut and the raised voices are just a murmur and the murmuring becomes just a whisper.

An hour passes and I can't sleep. I think of what they could be up to in the other room. I hear voices again, this time in anger, shouts and an occasional scream. A door is opened and slammed shut and Lisa wanders in and sits next to me on the settee.

'He's always mean,' she cries to me.

I sit up, put my arm around her and look into her eyes. A few complaints from her and a bit of understanding from me later, and I kiss her and it feels very right, even though he's in the next room.

Her boyfriend appears in the doorway as we part kissing for the third time, and he explodes with rage.

'Stand up, fuck!' he shouts, 'I'm going to kick the shit out of you!'

'Nasty,' I say, grinning and putting on a camp voice—I'm still very much drunk and stoned.

'Stand up, fuck, or I'll kick you sitting down.'

Lisa seems unmoved by the situation and looks at the floor.

'Nicky, calm down,' she says to him, still looking at the floor.

'Nicky? Nicky?' I say and start to crack up, stoned. Sniggering at first and then a proper laugh. He gets more enraged and animated and I notice a degree of campness to him that makes me laugh even more.

'Stand up!' he yells, shaking and flailing his arms about. He is camp, I decide; camp, very angry and cheated on by me, this drunk, caned, giggling man on his settee who, to top it all off, has just heard his girly name.

Nicky explodes into action, grabbing me by the wrist, trying to get me to stand. I just giggle and laugh at him, his name and the situation. It all feels right. He drags me off the settee across the living room into the hallway. All the time I laugh and occasionally say, 'Nasty man.' He struggles to open the door and shove me out into the hallway as I grab the door frame and handle. He manages eventually and, in the end, it doesn't feel right to put up a fight other than to take his side—it isn't a contest; the demons of my past would kill him. I'm better laughing it off.

Out in the hallway after the door has been slammed shut and I've tapped a few times to get back in, I collapse sideways against the wall to reflect for a while. I notice my watch strap is broken and whilst putting it in my pocket, I rediscover the brown envelope, lift it out and finish opening it.

Inside there's a single sheet of A4 with a single body of text made up of cuttings of photocopied letters. It's photocopied again and again so that the finished article is grainy and full of black overexposed lines. As I look at it, it steals my focus from the flat I've just been ejected from and the pain in my head that's starting to want to be a hangover. The note reads like a stream of consciousness, mentioning randomness, aggression, hysterical reactions, concrete veins, a life-sustaining stream and rejection.

My stoned, drunk and humiliated head throbs and I return the A4 sheet to the envelope, close it, and turn it over to check who it was meant for. It's addressed to me.

8

I sleep heavy again on my settee, when I get back. I sink into it like it's a giant upholstered blancmange, moulding to my mass, wrapping and hugging my limbs tight. This time I think I'm woken up by burglars looking for a ring, I just don't know for sure whether it happened or not.

'He lost his ring!' one of them says to me as I roll my head over to see them stood around in my sitting room.

'When we had that girl on your floor!' another says.

'When we took her,' the leader says. 'The ring,' he goes on, 'I want it back.' He looks angrily at me then turns and leaves. Two others leave after him and the last one takes his time, then looks back over his shoulder at me and the room.

'It's important—we're going to get it back. It was engraved, real personal like. We didn't know that bitch would claw it off of him,' he says over his shoulder.

'What does the engraving say?' I sleepily murmur.

'You know what it says, fuck... it says; Love Nicky!' he finishes, and walks out.

I wake with a jump and stagger to the door to check it's shut and locked. With three hours before work, a painful head and the fear, I desperately need a drink.

9

It depends on how close to ground level you are whether you notice the hit coming or going. Ground level is in another building; I just work in a non-descript head office outlet, a machine. A machine for thoughtless unquestioning obedience—it's a machine for dogs.

On my way out to work, in the corridor and approaching the front door I notice a brown envelope again, not yet fallen and caught in the letter box flap. I take it, open the door against the mass of envelopes piled on the floor, and leave for work. The envelope is another saved treat for later as I read it out loud, and its madness will inevitably mirror my own growing madness and unease with my predicament that seems to be this, my new life and being.

I tell my dream from the night before to my work colleague sat next to me, and again he offers some sort of divine insight, and again I hate it.

'I fell asleep on the settee and had one of those, you know, waking dreams. I dreamt I woke up and was surrounded by burglars looking for something, a ring,' I say.

'Rings represent eternity, or eternal life,' he says, 'and the burglars, they're the bad side of you that's lost your eternal life,' preaching on, 'as you look on, literally helpless, from your sleepy haze just sat lazing on your busted old settee of a life!'

'Coffee?' I ask.

At the coffee machine I take out the brown envelope I have in my back pocket. Again it's a faded, sketchy photocopy of a photocopied cut-up document, talking in a stream of consciousness. It mentions a stream cut short, abruptness, something uncomfortable, travelling hysteria and a degeneration of the self. I return the note to the envelope and hold it in the hand with the cup. My friend's coffee is ready now, but not quite. I tip a bit out, undo my fly and begin to top it up with my piss.

'JASON!' a shout comes from behind me and I turn to face my boss as I still strain to give the Christian the last little taste of my liquid insight.

'Stream cut short,' I say abruptly. 'Very uncomfortable!'

'What?!' my boss says, glancing between my glazed-over expression and my hand, with letter, dick and the cup not quite full but close enough.

'Degeneration into true self,' I say and the letter falls to the ground.

I shake off: I am finished.

10

'Breakdown... Break free more like!' I say, as the concluding line in my lengthy handwritten defence to my very short-term employer. A bitter twisted irony at the end of thirty-five pages of apparently sycophantic drivel. They drank it all up until the last line spat so fiercely in the face of it all. They hate that, being understood and played at their own game by someone who's been there so little time.

It's a simple play though; I knew the lines to it pretty quick; it's not rocket science. The man at the top calls the shots and the rest scramble round for credit, fucking over whoever they can to get near him with the next fucking PowerPoint slideshow of pure crap. Their faces say it all before their mouths do. They hate my resignation letter. Made worse by reading and nodding their way through it, unexpectant, as I'm sat coyly with a seriously stony face opposite them. Then they get to the fingers up bit I've written at the end, 'Breakdown...break free more like!' And I just grin and wink—they deserve something, just. So, I give it to them.

'A mental breakdown brought on by excess alcohol and a meandering mind,' my boss and his superior say to me from the other side of the big oval boardroom table. 'You're suspended from duties pending an ongoing review of the situation and your progress. Pay is halved.'

'Fuck you and your dog machine,' I say and there's their response. I leave, secretly quite grateful of the half-pay for doing nothing. The protection programme I'm on must have some weight from authorities even higher than them. The money I will treat as a dull corporate sponsorship, maybe to do another trade, or if being more honest with myself, just piss away up the wall. I'm grateful, and a cheap drunk.

I decide to still walk towards work every morning at nine, not to go in but to follow Lisa the photocopier girl; she has a good sway, hips, tits and all—it's something to do.

The brown envelopes arrive every two or three days, and every time they do, I'm there on the other side of the letter box waiting for them. It's as if we're in tune with each other. I know their cycle as if I'd designed it myself. I decide the cryptic messages are the machine taunting me from a distance. The machine manipulates me. It formed me (inside), it fired me and now it controls me like a master puppeteer.

A portcullis drops down around my feelings and I have no worries or emotions, stone cold. The letters are free to become my rules, become my god! Trapped in my protection, sacked from my job, my emotional detachment from people, family and friends is at a height now.

If I die now, it will be the first time I truly experience the loss of someone.

11

I should have retreated to recover, reset and restart myself. I should have gone home, home whilst I still had one, but I didn't. I stayed in the flat and drank, drank like a bastard and I waited. And so this is how it started over again, a new beginning, being reborn—maybe by mistake. I sat at the table looking out of the window on Sunday morning, with the morning sun stinging my dazed hangover behind the eyes. Then it arrived, a little brown envelope slipped quietly and slowly under my door. In roughly the same format as the previous ones, only this time it had the seed that would grow into my new purpose in only a few minutes' time. I just didn't know it yet...

I opened the plain brown envelope with shaking hands. I was a breakfast drink or two off settling them back down again. With one end open, I tipped the contents out and a single sheet of headed A4 fell out. In the middle of the page was scribbled 'knock knock—he's coming!' Slightly less cryptic and more intriguing than the previous notes. This one was more direct and had a clue to there being more to it than an idle drunken mad scrawl that I may or may not have sent to myself, to relieve my boredom when I had a job. This one had an agenda, and a clear source. It was headed with a Celtic Manor Hotel stamp but wasn't addressed on the envelope so must have been delivered by the author, or someone running for them.

Then it came…

KNOCK. KNOCK. As loud as life, rap rap, on the door and I pause, waiting, waiting to be reborn into my new life like a half-drunken bedraggled ape ready to be shot at the sun. Not knowing what's in store, I could shrivel up, scared and anxious, but I don't. I stand up and walk towards the door to answer it and feel something stir that hasn't been around in a while. I feel a drive towards the unknown, and any danger that could come with it. I feel a pulse stir as though I'm waking for the first time.

I open the door to reveal the arguing Irishman from upstairs. He's panting and his eyes dart around the door frame without settling on me. Words start to come from his mouth sounding almost rehearsed, like he'd been practising them before he came down to try them out on me. Maybe that's just how it seems when someone hits you with something like that, with such drama. We're used to just reading it or hearing it in the movies, so a natural British instinct is to be the cynic, suspicious and on the defence, I guess. His lack of eye contact might be panic or dishonesty. As I begin to think more about it, I realise I'm perfectly silhouetted in the door frame with the morning sun beating and streaming around me from the windows behind— he's blinded by the sun.

'She's gone,' he says. 'I don't know what to do, it's been days.'

'Where do I fit into this?' I let out, already suspecting I'm part of a bigger picture. The to and fro of him stating his predicament and me looking suspicious and quizzical continues for some time, way beyond the call of duty for a doorstep chat between unsociable neighbours. It's clear he's not going anywhere and isn't waiting for sympathy; he's building up to something he wants from me. And then it comes. An offer from him and a chance of a new start for me. He's given me enough time for my mind to wander and then it comes to me, how I can use this whole situation.

'I think I need some help—you're the first door I've come to,' he says, again no eye contact until he's finished. Then he gives me a glance to see how he's being received, and to see if his shit sticks.

'Who are you anyway—what are you?' he asks.

'John Barrie. I'm a de..." I pause, and my brain reorganises itself, resets, and I stop saying 'designer' mid-word, and it is reformatted and so in turn is my life, irreversibly, forever. 'I'm a detective. A private detective...an investigator, a PI.' And it feels like a test to myself as much as to him as the words leave my lips.

It's pretentious at best, and if it's taken for just a lie even better. It would take practice, no doubt and by the time I'm used to saying it, I won't need to or I'll be pushed onto the next self-invention from my boredom.

'You're a fucking drunk,' he stabs in the air with his words and physically into my chest with his finger, shattering any delusions of grandeur before my new self has even walked the street.

'I need something to do between one case and another,' I say. 'A way to wipe the slate clean and start again on a new one. Maybe yours? I've seen a lot of shit, and it needs to be gotten rid of. I'm not an Irish Catholic so the bottle's my confessional.'

He stiffens up at this and I sense I might be touching too many nerves with each stinking breath he must be able to smell, hence his comment, and the words carried on them. He's asking for help, he's come to me, there's a missing girl and I've said I'm a detective.

I wonder if he's buying all this, that this has just all come together and it being fate I'm this convenient detective between cases and his neighbour. Surely he's a fool if he does. Maybe, and maybe not. He could be playing me? If so, I have just offered myself up to him as a fool myself and played right into his hands, and more than he could have possibly hoped for. He then reaches into his back pocket with his right hand but leaves it there as if he came prepared to make some kind of offer but wasn't going to show his hand just yet. But, as he does, I realise he has shown his hand anyway. As any poker player will tell you: don't reach for the chips, not at all, unless you want people to think you're committed. Don't reach for the chips too soon, giving your game away. Unless they're out of sight and the players can't see how much you're going for. You might have nothing in the first place but your bluffing them and suggesting you do with the gesture. Be sure you're going to win or bluff. If you're going to do it, be sure to go all the way.

'I'll find her,' I say.

'Here's a grand and a half.' He stares at me, pushing the brown envelope into my chest. And I know this just isn't how it's meant to work. I hadn't even considered money and if I had, I'd have been thinking five hundred tops, and then maybe some more when done. That is if she's even alive and glad to be found in the first place.

This isn't how I would have thought this would work, and if it is, then I should have had a drunken breakdown sooner. So I chance it—after all, if I'm on the case then he's my first client, that and my first suspect. What with the arguments and her mysteriously disappearing, and now him on my doorstep after an envelope cued his arrival so neatly with a scribbled 'knock knock'.

'I'll need a car, or money to hire one,' I chance. Again giving too much away—a fool, or taking me for one—his left hand goes into his left pocket and this time takes out a set of keys; still staring, he dangles them in front of me. I reach out my hand staring back.

'Red Saab, outside, I want it back. I want it and her… back!'
And he drops the keys into my hand. Not a question, not a query
on why I thought I'd need a car, not a negotiation on money,
offering more for her back or less upfront. He was top of my hit
list already and if I was going to get played by anyone, I'd have
to figure this out and end up on top of the situation, the game.

Meanwhile I had new purpose, a new person to be. I knew I
needed the car, and maybe he did too really. I needed the car to
drive down past the hospital, up the M32, past Fishponds and
the shitty trading estates, past the mosque on the right as it turns
into dual carriageway and out of Bristol. John Barrie was going
down the M4 corridor westbound, over the bridge, paying his
toll, and on to that big fucking corporate golfing politician hell
hole, that giant complex the Celtic Manor Hotel—as headed on
the notepaper.

He grabs me by the throat and I haven't considered yet
whether I'm a hard drinking, hard smoking, toughened PI yet.
One that doesn't take any shit. Or maybe I'm the type that's
grateful of a new client's cash and would willingly take any
roughing up first, whilst knowing I have an escape. But maybe
I'm the kind that feels better with someone needing something
from me.

'I'm Sean, by the way,' he says, still holding my windpipe
firmly. Sean the Bastard, I think, whilst remembering all the
times I've heard him shouting at her; the screams, and maybe
more physical stuff besides. Yes Sean the Bastard, and his grip
tightens and confirms it.

'Don't forget,' he says, "I know where you live.'

The Irish are such happy types normally. The stuff of idle
banter, jokes on life and meandering happy-go-lucky
conversationalists avoiding the harsh shit of real life. But, take

them out of their natural habitat, deprive them of Guinness and whiskey for a couple of years, and put them in a hole of a rented third-floor flat in Bristol and the bitterness soon takes over. All that while living on Lower Park Row close enough to Clifton to smell the money but also on the doorstep of the hospital and Broadmead, living a hand-to-mouth existence, deep in the despair and emergency room of the city around them. We're all the same really, fighting for what we want, living with what we'll put up with, and never with what we actually need or desire.

I shut the door real slow, giving him the chance to take his hand from my throat. He removes it slowly enough to make the point that strangling me could happen whether there was a door in the way or not. After all, he knows where I live, Sean, Sean the Bastard. I walk back over to the table in front of the window and sit down to inspect both envelopes, one of cash and another a warning or a clue—I haven't decided yet. Behind me the door is closed but I can hear Sean breathing there behind it.

'The answers to the questions you should have asked me are with the cash,' he taunts through the door. 'Private Detective...' he finishes sarcastically. Regardless of what I am, what I said I am or what I am reinventing for myself, he knew I was there. He came prepared and he knew what I was to him, a patsy and a scapegoat to play out his game.

I had my corporate sponsor, an envelope of cash from a mad Irishman, a car and a reason to hit the road. I want to play this out, I think, for better or worse. After all, I should have got myself better again, recuperated; I really should have gone back home, back home when I still had one.

I opened an end of the envelope Sean gave me, white this time, with a window for an address that wasn't needed. I tip out the contents: a bundle of fifties, a Polaroid and some notepaper with childish scribbles on it hit the table.

Sean was a tall, dark and handsome man in a way. He looked like a pop star, hair starting to thin on the sides and back, a metrosexual with over-attention to grooming; fashion conscious down to the laces in his shoes. All this, but what was totally absent within his person was any true class, thoughtfulness beyond himself or to be considerate to a partner judging by all the arguing I'd heard through the walls and ceilings.

Sean the Bastard was Sean Ballard, I knew this already from the mounting bills on the door mat by the communal flats' entrance. His girl was Cherry O' Neill. He'd scrawled this down, maybe manically, panicking and scared, or maybe because he wasn't used to writing anything other than the occasional guilty greetings cards to an estranged relative over the water. The photo was of them together, both posing, both oozing vanity. Him looking happy as she's on his arm looking good and because it completes his look. Her pretending to look happy for the sake of completing the pretty photo in her head, and to show her friends she's trying to look the part. Vacuous and swallowing each other's souls to the core.

I was going to hit the road, but first I was going to drive fifty yards up the road to the petrol station and then I was going to drive another fifty to the White Harte, a pub I'd been previously stumbling to and from for some time. This time I'd pull up in style, of sorts, and I'd drink to settle down my nerves for the task in hand. After all it didn't seem right to approach Wales without a protective layer or albeit a short-lived beer jacket that in reality wouldn't stop a child with a jelly spoon. The self-delusion wheels were turning and I needed to think out my game plan and my new invented identity as it was creeping over me.

I brush the contents back into the envelope with my elbow, careful not to touch anything directly. I put on my only sorry suit, thinking how bizarre it is that this scruffy office skin is so easily transferable in appearance to the rained-on, downtrodden detective look I have in mind.

I have a moment's thought for the other transferable elements I am going to employ over the next few days. Not least the over-analysis of the self, the human condition in tatters, my own, and others'. In fact, it has already well and truly started, for I was already in the head of Sean, Sean the Bastard, just like a drunken little wood worm. And Cherry, well I'd been in there, thinking of her for some time.

The Saab, a once red but now sun-bleached, tarnished lipstick shade, had several tickets on its windscreen and set a tone for its disregard that I was going to continue by adding myself into it.

I drive the short distance to the petrol station and pick up a handful of plastic gloves. Then I drive an equally short distance to the front of the White Harte and pull up outside on the double yellows. I get out slowly, looking over the car roof at the pub, hoping to be noticed and feeling like a footballer leaving a Ferrari.

It had been raining and a truck drives behind me, clattering through a puddle and spraying muddy water over me and the car. A wasted attempt by me to be noticed, I realise when I enter the pub, sodden in muddy water.

The pub is dead except for a man on his own, sat with his head down scribbling into a notebook in the corner. The sun comes through the windows silhouetting him—similar to my previous attempt at an epiphany image of myself, with Sean in my own doorway.

I order two pints, down one and then sit close enough to him to try and see what he's scribbling, without actually seeing anything. A timid start to my new role of investigator, and he wasn't even part of it, he was just a stranger in a pub working, writing, or trying to look like as if he is waiting to pick up someone—just an academic peacock flashing his tail feathers. His Moleskine might have been full of idle shit for all I could see. So I got closer, half to practise spying and half just for something to do.

'Yes?' he says, noticing me straight away. 'Can I help you?'

'I'm John.'

'And I'm busy!' he returns fire at me.

'What you busy at?' And the back and forth continues for an uncomfortable amount of time. I soften him eventually by pretending to give up, returning to my pint on the table and then quietly getting my own little black book out and starting to scribble in it. The curiosity gets the better of him. A useful tool; let the fish come to you, jump on the hook. A little bit of mirroring goes a long way to pandering to an ego.

'Sorry, I didn't realise you were a writer too,' he says, offering his olive branch and then continuing with an onslaught of words and what feels a bit like being shot with a CV. He was an austere kind of character to talk to so far, called Paul Benjamin. An author on his first book, dabbling with noir, both real and fictional by the sounds of it.

'Of sorts, I guess. I'm am writing, yes, so a writer,' I say.

'I've just moved my scribbling to this White Harte here, in Clifton. I was in the Bedminster one before. Spelt without the e, you know?'

'Why did you change?' I ask, ignoring his pub name trivia.

'Would have killed me.'

'Really?!'

'I'm writing about a down-and-out drunken detective, and it made sense to put him there in that lowlife street in a dead-end kind of pub. Then surround him by people on or close to the edge.'

'Makes sense, although they're here too though you know? You might be with one now.'

'Yes maybe. Different kind, I guess, less teeth and more literary!'

'Why then, why did you move?' And I show him a little teeth with a mini snarl.

'Because they were on or too close to the edge. Nearly had me—animals and heathens the lot of them.'

'Makes sense.'

'And it does, you see. To put a character like that, over there, in my writing. But maybe I'm not suited to gonzo writing, or, maybe what works well to read, and is entertaining, just isn't really liveable—not really and not real.'

'Oh it's real enough,' I say, with the morning's events to confirm it.

'Really? What brings you here, and what are you writing?'

'I'm a lowlife drunken detective on my first case and trying to get my head and balls together to make it past the starting line, to get to the end. You picked the right pub this time.' I say, 'It's not a retreat to safety. Good luck.'

And I finish up, down what's left of my drink and leave, thinking about how I am, in fact, living this. This, and his fiction. This is all real enough to me. My form follows a fiction.

12

I hit the road, on the way to the M32 out of Bristol, but I just have to make one small stop first: another pub, this time in deepest, darkest Bristol, or that's what the estate agents would have you believe.

Bordering the St Paul's and Montpelier regions of the city, the Star & Garter has an open all hours, boarded-up, permanent lock-in policy and, as a result, many a soul has been lost and found there, searching for themselves in a drink and drugs haze. A waiting room for the city's wasted to get back on the life train, and a genuine challenger to the local church for a real working community service.

I'd been there a few times, mostly in error, leaving a club on the bottom of Stokes Croft in the early hours of the morning, and drunkenly turning right instead of left. It wouldn't appear on the tourist trail for another ten years, but now, in the late nineties, it still belonged to this dirty part of the city and its members that it regularly shat back out onto the street. Usually, this happened on a Monday morning when they realised they had a job to go to, still swimming high in a pot-smoked cloud.

Today was no different and, as I pulled up, the shutters were predictably down. The graffiti on the corner of the building would take other ten years to be considered art, and in fact worth more than the pub itself. So with the kicked-over bins, a drunk lying in his takeaway spoils, and the growing smell of weed on this Sunday afternoon, I locked up the lipstick-coloured, faded red Saab. I went into the Star & Garter, a church to the lost, and a real place to find answers to life's questions and maybe the whereabouts of Cherry.

I knocked on the door, and it opened. If I could see through the smoke I'd see a black, dreaded barman with a beard. I knew he was there because I got let in. He was as much a part of the building as the building was of Bristol. If he wasn't there, it wouldn't be open. If he wasn't there, the pub wouldn't be there. Symbiotic pub, city and man working together for the people.

On the other hand, if you could smell through the weed, you'd wish you couldn't. People didn't come here to be looked at, judged; white or black, clean or if they'd soiled themselves.

DJ Derek was here spinning some reggae in the corner; a little white old pensioner DJing on a Sunday afternoon to a handful of night beforers who hadn't seen daylight since Friday. He's another beloved treasure of the city, like the barman, Brunel's suspension bridge or Turbo Island, the tiny patch of grass which harbours the traffic-baiting drunks and punks of Stokes Croft.

'Ah, man, ah.' The barman welcomes me through the sweet mist, and I'm not sure if he should recognise me or not, greeting me like a friend as he did all his patrons. I head towards the voice in the smoke and lean against the bar which is wet, but I am too, so it's of little concern; just layers of wet beer on beer sweat.

'You seen a girl in here?' I ask to the smoke.

'Drink first?' he asks, and I sense crossed wires.

'No, no, but yes, rum,' and it lands in front of me almost as quickly as the words have finished leaving my mouth. Dark and like syrup, neither one shot nor two but more like three, free poured like you might do as one old friend to another. I scramble in my right trouser pocket and put a screwed-up fiver on the top, which in turn is snapped away, disappearing into his pocket and swapped for a two-pound coin.

'Cherry... She hangs around with an Irish fella normally?'

'Nah, man, but Cherry... red hair maybe.'

'There's enough cherry-red hair in this single mum part of town!'

'Aye, there's that.'

'I've seen the Irishman and the girl.' A different voice joins in, coming from behind me, lower down on a bench in the corner. I nod to the smoke cloud behind the counter and head towards where the voice was coming from. A glass or bottle hits me straight in the forehead as I'm halfway across the floor, and I don't know if it's in my eyes.

I've seen someone get glassed before a few times and it's debateable whether you're better off it breaking or not. The fist that followed knocked me straight to the floor and before I knew it, there were two sets of hands on my collar and neck, dragging me back out where I'd come from to outside, the light and impact stinging my eyes and head.

I don't know how long they kicked me for but I heard enough reference to Sean and the girl to know that they, or people asking after them, weren't welcome around these parts. How they didn't know I was a policeman or someone on their side told me something about how to carry myself into the next similar situation I found myself in.

'Can one of you bring my rum out? I hadn't finished,' I manage to get out before the last foot lands, as I lie on my side in amongst the wheelie bins with their contents spewed over me. A second later, one of them returns to throw it in my face, and I'm left grateful a match didn't follow behind it to set alight to my shameful exit. Not a great start for someone pretending to be a PI, but it was a learning exercise.

Firstly, Sean and Cherry are known in this friendly drug den of a church and friendly people turn into hostile animals at the mere mention of their names. Secondly, I could hold my temper, knowing when to hold back and take a beating. I assumed immediately that Irish Sean was involved in drug dealing and treading on people's toes on this side of town. I'm not the first to come looking for them and they're protecting them and him.

Or more worryingly and more likely, they just didn't like the look of me and were bored, so used me to dust off their shoes. I wasn't going to go in for a second round, in either sense, so I pick myself up, ashamedly looking in the rubbish as I stand up. There is a half-drunk bottle of something that looks like piss; I decide to leave it.

The car feels like a safety blanket as I open the door and collapse into the driver's seat exhausted. I insert the key, look at my trembling hands and as I look up, the front door of the pub crashes open and both of my new pals run towards the car. One has a bat and the other is reaching into a jacket pocket for something. When his hand emerges I can see it's a gun and it's pointed straight at the windscreen.

I can see they have both been rolled recently too and my kicking makes more sense. The last 'Cherry pickers' in there must have been a little less subtle than me maybe? They both stop in front of the car, and as the smoke clears I can see their angry faces mouthing 'fuck off and go', whilst waving with their spare hands. That's enough for me to leave and I put it in reverse, edging backwards, nodding and give them the peace sign with my hand on the wheel. The car slips out of gear, grinding and grunting. I force it back in, pull forward and as I turn I can see them laughing and slapping their legs like they'd played some sort of prank.

I'm tempted to return back to the White Harte, the safe one in Clifton; not Bedminster. Tempted to retreat back and write about it all instead and see the story out safely in my head. Just Paul Benjamin and me sat safely, drinking pints and musing over our Bristol Noir escapades. I stay committed to finding the girl; this is real and I am being reborn into this from my otherwise nothing of a life I'd been given. I'd need another drink though, and despite surprising myself in surviving the beating, I wasn't back to being as tough as I needed to be yet. Because I knew if I'd played a different hand and hadn't ended up rum soaked and beaten in the bins, no one might have and we could all have been sitting around together now chatting it out. I wouldn't have given away all my hand and game away so quickly either. I learnt that one in the first act from Sean's mistakes earlier, I think. Just like in poker, let them come to you before you show anything, if at all.

I stop at the services at the bottom of the M32, the one before you really get out of the city at all, and buy a bottle of whiskey and some cans. Why they sell that stuff in service stations I don't know, but they do and I'm glad. I return to the car, open a can with my spare hand and steer out of the forecourt onto the dual carriageway and towards the next lesson in my new persona.

As I drive down the dual carriageway heading out of Bristol, I hit a sudden wall of green either side of the road. The same happens pretty much if you walk in any direction out of the city too. It just stops dead, and the countryside hits you. There's no sprawl, ghetto or disused high-rises, it just stops and the lush pastures, woodlands, and if you head west, waterways and hills as far as the coast roll on and on.

Bristol's beauty is it isn't a city as people typically know it. Its intersections with Avonmouth, the riverways and the gorge have it kept constantly in check with nature; both the urban and rural pushing and pulsating back and forth. It's a great feeling to leave, with the illusion of getting fresh air in the lungs and greenery, even better to return to and realise it's ingrained in the city anyway.

On the passenger seat, the envelope Sean had given me was starting to burn an impression on my mind, and the further I got, the more I wanted to be into it. I reach across, still looking at the road, empty out the money with the photo of him and Cherry, and whilst holding it up to the steering wheel, I fold it over so I can just see her.

As the second can sinks effortlessly into my bloodstream the respite from the hangover lifts and the euphoria commences, and with this, the hangover horn rears its ugly head. I touch the picture, pawing at it with a finger and trying to concentrate on the road. It was no good; I hadn't wanked or fucked in some time. If I was passing a services at this time I'd have pulled over and I'd be in there, walking straight past the coffee, donuts, tents for sale, the old lady handing out leaflets for God, tools, inflatables and magazines and heading straight to the nearest toilet cubical to pull at myself like a frenzied chimp, and then I'd leave. There wasn't a services in wankable distance though, so I steer on with an itch I couldn't scratch. My shame is left physically intact except for the gnawing intent pushing at my zip from the inside.

I drive further north to the Severn crossing on the M48 and it's getting late in the afternoon by the time I get close to the bridge to Wales. I pass a pair of arguing lovers, wrapped inside each other's lies, manically battling on the other side by a Vauxhall Cavalier. I think how lucky I am to have found a way forward for now.

I know I've found a way and a purpose out of the boredom

and idle drinking—the boredom anyway. All before it's got to a point where I can't operate any more as a human being, and before I can't reach the bar without something going badly wrong, or my body is too weak to walk.

Like a piss-soaked black butterfly emerging from a cocoon, I push on over the bridge feeling like I'm establishing my transformation into my true self. Gliding in the clouds, railings flying past and the sea lapping below, I stick my head out the window and, with one hand on the wheel, I feel more than a few cobwebs getting blasted out of me.

I pull something close to a growing smile and feel something trickle down my face and realise I have what's left of a nosebleed from the kicking earlier. Returning my head to the car I look in the mirror and see the little black hard tributaries of old hardened blood, with a fresh little stream tickling down to the corner of my mouth. I lick the back of my hand, wipe at my face and it feels good; I'm on a case, and I have the marks to prove it.

I need to get cleaned up a bit if I am going to act out the next chapter of this though, unless my part is that of a sick tramp needing a room for the night who happens to have an envelope stuffed with cash. Remembering the cash, I put on a plastic glove and whilst steadying the wheel, I pick up a bundle of the notes and tease a couple of them out from under the elastic band that's holding them together. I then put them up to the windscreen. Clearly they weren't all going to be fakes, and not all real either. Just like my little act. Good job the corporate sponsorship is there in the background, I think, whilst removing the glove and dropping it with the notes to the seat.

The wind pushes in through the window, tossing the notes, dancing them around the car. I ignore it a while then think a little further into their twist; the top note on the pile was real and the rest fake, of course. I decide to keep the stack and get by the best I can without using them; after all I might need all the evidence I can get against Sean the Bastard. I hadn't dirtied my hands yet.

I steer my way off the motorway which winds down, round and under itself like a mini spaghetti junction, driving on to the main entrance of the Celtic Manor Hotel. As I do, my mind ticks over the events leading up to this point; the missing girl, the dodgy boyfriend who beats her, his questionable reputation in the Star & Garter pub and what I am going to find here at this hotel? More trouble or another series of events just pointing toward Sean actually just being a bastard?

The headed notepaper which led me here may have originated here, but it was delivered by hand. Then my subconscious takes over, and I think: If she wrote the note warning you, then she must still be in Bristol, near the flats, maybe close enough to know when he was coming and going, and me too. Face it, John Barrie, your new persona just fancied a little trip to earn your packet of fake fifties, fake money from the Irishman to get a fake you out of the city and your mind.

'We'll see,' I say to myself, and, 'I like the cut of this new skin, I'll see this through in Newport, Bristol or anywhere else it takes me.' I was cutting my teeth on this first case, and would come out on top or just fall back into the gutter with my beer-rotten soul.

I sit in the car, staring up at the big corporate beast of a hotel where everyone from prime ministers, presidents, pop stars and the red-carpet parade had fucked, pissed, slept and golfed away our taxes and respect. I would need to strap on a pair before I entered, so I down the last can and leave a little to wet my hands and run through my hair.

Then I ponder my angle, another name to use maybe, or test

the water with how much authority an investigative title could hold. I stop overthinking it, open the car door and launch myself at the building. I walk with confidence and certainty, which I am sure was going to count for half the act I'd need anyway.

The automatic doors hiss open to reveal a grand reception lobby with a tall circular ceiling, which I pretend not to notice, like I stay in places like this all the time. I coolly navigate my way towards the main desk where all illusions, acts and pretences are shattered by a stern battleaxe of a woman who looks at me over her thick-rimmed glasses like a school teacher might inspect dog shit in a kids' playground.

This is why all women should be in positions of power. They can smell a rat, act, ego or misdirection a mile off. They're designed for it and in a comment, look or small gesture, can cut it down to size. She looks like she's been dealing with crap all her life, is used to it. A hardened long-timer.

'You look like you're with the group that's just left. Forgotten something have we?' she asks coldly.

'No, just arrived.'

'Thank god. You don't know them at all then?'

'No.'

'Well, you do look like them, the men anyway. Like some of the women too.' And she gives me a bit of relief and humour in her voice. I hadn't talked down at her or shouldered any bravado yet, so she was on side for now. She hasn't decided if I'm a prick, not yet.

'I'm intrigued. What happened? What corporate coach load hit you last?'

'I'll tell you, sonny,' she says like I'm the three-year-old, now playing with that turd in the playground. 'Some corporates from over the water, a late or early Christmas do. Hard to tell these days. It was like Sodom!'

I lean forward to take it in. I'd love to hear some dirt on anything that sounds like the company I've been capsized from. And as she goes on I realise it actually is the same company; the one I've been suspended from.

'Room 73 will never be the same again! Dirty filth all over the walls, floors and bedding. These people are meant to be professionals.'

She's obviously been waiting to offload the weekend's gossip and frustrations at someone and I was taking the first load gladly. 'Poor Steve's still cleaning the escalator; it ran right into the bottom step and into the workings of it, you know?'

'Really?' I lean forward more, over the desk.

'And that was the girls!'

'What?'

'Girls, yes. Squatting on the top step and using it like a drunken hen do might on the fountain steps back on Bristol waterfront!'

'Room 73?' I fish for more.

'Yes, it's taken them all morning to clean it out—I can't bring myself to say exactly what. And these are married people. They've got other halves, you know, and they just treat it all like a no rules…'

'A swingers' Butlin's,' I finish her sentence for her.

'Yes, and we have important people stay here, you know! In fact the President of the United States only last month—he was such a lovely, lovely man!'

'Did he shit the bed too?'

She splutters, half in agreement, then turns her stern eyes back on me, just in case I was making fun of her. I wasn't though, I was quite serious.

'Anyway, Mr…?'

'Bowie,' I say, picking a new surname for myself. 'I'm staying for a night or two, maybe longer.' The use of the Bowie name wouldn't be the first time it had been used for some commercial gain. A pop star and a knife company had milked it and now I would. 'Yes. Mr J Bowie, for a couple of nights. I'm here to meet Cherry.'

'Ah yes, I see we're expecting you,' she says, looking at a sheet of A4 on the desk and I hide my surprise and take it that she's in on something. The name Bowie isn't different enough from Barry, not different enough in this situation anyway to catch someone out; not a sharp, hawk-eared woman like this. Fact is the meeting Cherry was probably the little piece she was waiting for and expecting. I can see enough over the counter to see the sheet of A4 she pretended to scan is in fact blank.

'I didn't book.'

'You didn't have to. Here's your key! Number 73, up the escalator on the seventh floor,' she says, not looking up and putting it on the counter top. She gives me the filth room she had just been referring to, with a playful and evil half-grin on her face. Hearing the hiss of the automatic doors of her next check-ins, she points and ushers me out of her way with an index-finger wave, all whilst peering over my shoulder again with her schoolteacher-on-patrol look.

I hope for their sake they're liberal vegetarian lesbians. They won't be though, and she'll get her pound of flesh, her revenge on some old corporate sucker for the filthy bastards that preceded them.

I bypass the escalator, head for the bar and take a stool next to the shiny chrome pumps. Everything in here is shiny, leather and buffed with a handful of 'on brand' coloured cushions to tie it all together—crass interior decorating by a machine, for machines. I don't have much to check in to the room except myself, an envelope of copied fifties and a white Moleskine notebook, and so I'm not in any hurry to freshen up even if I should be. I prop up the bar and sit it out, thinking over my route so far, the events and the cast of characters that might be involved in the hotel, including the dragon of a woman on the reception desk.

At first it didn't take long—after all it could only really be Sean the Bastard who's checked me in, or the writer of the note, or Cherry, who could be one and the same person. And who's to say Cherry wrote anything and Sean didn't fiddle the whole caper himself, with Cherry bound up or worse back in their flat?

I order a drink, putting it to the room and, as I do the barman makes a face of acknowledgement at the room number of filth. His glance tells me more than the dragon at the front desk did— the true horror of it all. What it didn't tell me though, is if he thought I was a part of it or if he just felt sorry for me.

After a second or third handful of nuts from the bowl on the bar, I remember the dragon's story about the escalator and room. Suddenly I wonder how long the nuts have been on the bar, with all the dirty little corporate claws the night before scooping in for a handful after having thumbed each other's holes to tatters.

I put the remaining nut that's in my hand back into the bowl, pick up the envelope, notebook, a hotel-branded pen from a pot on the bar and head to a seat in the corner of the room. There's a big TV overhead showing a news article about India conducting atomic tests despite worldwide disapproval. Pakistan has staged five nuclear tests in response. And in Iraq, UN arms inspectors are attempting to do their jobs and not getting anywhere. They won't, and Clinton will bomb us all into the next decade and more.

13

I think everyone I've ever known, loved or hated goes away in the end, and by then it's just me against the dust and drink.

A sharp silhouette snaps me out of my morose drunken thoughts, snapping me back into the room. She's unavoidable and, as I look up away from the table top at the slender 5'6" black dress that's gliding in, it smells like a perfume grenade has been tossed into the room—filling the air, stealing everyone's attention from wherever it was previously.

I notice her and about three other sad males sat alone pretending to be busy in their own little worlds too. She could have taken her pick if she wanted to, but she didn't. She sat with her back to the room on a bar stool, waiting for the inevitable; of course the sadness of the room would come to her. It's embarrassing and I stay out of it.

Men order drinks to their table and one for her at the bar, again and again it happens. All this goes on with them, hopeful she'll turn round and come over to thank them; like she would be in a debt of some kind and owe them. Men are true shit. She drinks the offerings and stays fixed to her spot at the bar; like a bored queen, the sycophants lapping at her, throwing grapes into her mouth as she idles in her bathtub like Cleopatra.

There are two types of men when it comes to approaching lone pretty women in bars. The shit type and the don't-have-the-balls-to-be-a-shit jealous type, and I was the latter. And in situations like this, the prey becomes the hunter and it's all just an under-stocked meat market trading in egos, tits and shame. I was kidding myself really, I don't have the nerves at the moment and am in a limbo, drunken zombie-like state so I decide to play a different game.

I leave the room, head out to the car whilst hoping to create an air of lacking some interest in her, therefore differentiating myself from them, or an air that I'm so important I have to be somewhere else. I sit in the cocoon that is a lipstick shade of Saab in the car park and then down a quarter of the bottle of whiskey, slap myself in the face and return to the hotel bar feeling ten feet tall. I sit back down and write in my notebook ignoring the room; all of the male shits in it and her. The line was thrown out to sea, and she bites like a beautiful, blue, sleek marlin...

'Bukowski was a prick!' she says, looking down at me, having walked over from the bar. 'But at least he kept his selfish scribbles private!'

She had me, my act, my ego (or lack of it) and saw through to my core straight away. I love women; they're some kind of magic; something to be both respected and revered. If you can keep them on side, you are unstoppable.

'I think you're giving more credit to my scribbles than is due,' I say as a surrender of wills on my part. 'At least Bukowski saw fit to send his work out into the world in the end. I'd happily be seen writing in the corner. Not having the actual writing leave the room, seen or heard.'

'Why? Because it's too good, or too bad?' she asks.

'It's figuring something out and until I know who's in it, I'll keep it close to my chest.'

'Before you hit the big time?'

'No. The players of the game already know they're in and they don't need me to tell them that.'

'Drink? Actually, let's make it a few drinks. I like you already,' she asks and answers for me all at once. She stands up, then hip-sways herself to the bar. All eyes are on us and one corporate whore shakes his head mouthing words of disbelief. I mouth an angry mime of 'Fuck Off and Die!' and hold the look at them like an animal they aren't used to. Their eyes simply retreat back into the shells they came from when they realise the madness in me. I'm not one of them, I'm not playing the same game and their rules don't apply.

People come and go, cigarettes are lit then put out and nuts tossed in the air and eaten. Some of the corporate types end up together after a few drinks, bonding over a football game on the TV screen. The room buzzes around us but we're fixed on each other, engaged in a battle of who can deprecate me more.

She obviously doesn't believe such a man can exist and keeps at it, prodding and goading me like a fisherman harpooning an already beached whale. Three drinks each and I realise I haven't paid for any (unless she's been putting it to my room), and I stand up to go to the toilet, balance myself on a chair back, then push onwards.

The toilets are a mass of beige tiles and stark spotlights everywhere. My reflection looks beaten and haggard for a man of twenty-seven and I am sure she's up to something, perhaps she's put something in me I hadn't bargained on. When I go back out, I decide to interrogate rather than stroke her prerogative. What was she really after and what was she really up to?

'You can't really have come here looking for someone like me to abuse?'

'No, just luck I suppose.'

'Lucky me, but really—what are you doing here?'

'I work here…'

'You don't look like a maid, receptionist, bouncer or golf caddy.'

'I said I work here, not for here. It's my base. Easy clients here; they come to me and they don't haggle either. Some of them are just happy for the company, you know?'

'Oh, I'm not looking for that,' I lie.

'Who's to say I'm offering? Anyway, it's my day off, you look interesting and I fancy some company for a few drinks,' she says, almost getting defensive, but she's tough and I don't even scratch the surface of her armour.

'Sorry, where were we? Bukowski's a prick and so am I…'

'Bukowski was, but you are one.' She smiles, cheekily this time and on my side with a wink.

'I'll get a drink—another Long Island Ice Tea was it? You really knock them back.' As I say it, I realise she isn't wobbly, slurring or showing any signs at all. There are five or six shots in a Long Island Ice Tea and we've had three each. Had I been more switched on I'd have gone back into suspicious mode, but I don't. She's played me very well, making me feel guilty at my last round of questioning, very well indeed, as I'm now on the back foot and going to the bar. I decide the whiskey I'd drunk earlier that gave me strength was just putting me at a disadvantage now. That and she could seriously stomach her drink, whilst my Dutch courage had turned me into an Irish (or Scotch) joke. I notice the onset of double vision as I lean on the bar and the Guinness tap appears to change from one tap to two and back again, all in the time it takes the barman to notice I've walked over.

'Same again?' he says, looking over my shoulder at her. I notice a small exchange of gestures and try to keep it for reference, then look back to examine what he's doing as he mixes the drinks. He mixes both in front of the mirror behind the bar, with his back to me blocking any view. Normally ordering a cocktail is full of such pomp and ceremony, particularly in a place like this. Not this time though, and alarm bells ring in my head.

He puts them down in front of me, and I offer him my room number which is in turn dismissed as apparently it's already taken care of. Everyone's in on it, I think; receptionist dragon, barman and this girl too. As I walk back over, I've a little time to think. Is this beer paranoia? How in on something are they all? Or is the look the girl and barman exchanged just a 'put it on my tab' kind of look, in which case, if I want to get anywhere, I should probably stop thinking and behaving like an arsehole.

Besides, we're both drinking the same—how could tampering with them possibly work? No sooner had I thought it and I was putting them on the table in front of us, she goes against convention and takes the one I've placed nearer me. The one with the blue straw, rather than the one I put in front of her with the red straw.

'Favourite colour,' she says, putting it to her lips, and with another flirt of a wink, she shatters any logical thought train I was on. I try desperately to remember the colour of her previous straws, but she licks her lips, blowing my thoughts away again. All other considerations other than her become futile; she's won.

The best femme fatale isn't the one that isn't detected, it's the one that is. The man helpless to care about it either way, instead offering himself up to the slaughter, prepared to take whatever comes just for a few seconds more and kidding himself that it's all okay. You'll take as much as you can before you hit a brick wall, or any conclusion you hadn't wished for that wasn't her. She's good, a professional; she worked here alright.

The lights dim around us. I don't know what crazy circadian rhythm rule means that when it gets dark we feel we should make places even darker still, but we all do. Mood settings and body clocks I guess. They don't have a light setting for drunken male, senseless and being controlled like a puppet by the devil's own strumpet. So they just dim the lights, which is good as I'm starting to grin inanely like an idiot and glaze over, wearing the mask of a man drunk and attempting to act sober. Everything about her becomes not what she's doing or saying, but how she is doing it. Like a sensual ballerina, each turn and pirouette is an action of her mouth, hair and tone of her voice, crumbling my feeble male demeanour. I don't stand a chance and I offer myself and my boat up to the siren to be shattered across the rocks.

I wake with my head up against my room door. The number 73 in roman numerals presses itself into my forehead as she's fumbling in my right trouser pocket for the key. She's even managing to do that in a suggestive way, like there's still hope I might get it up. Thing is, I've Scottish blood at heart somewhere in me, so she's probably right and like the fighters and scrappers of the dark streets of Glasgow I was born to fight, fuck and punch my way through life. And what a life it is, reinvented to protect my identity by the authorities and reinvented again by me to save what's left of my sanity. I obviously need to be near the front line to keep my head, since nothing too easy in life seems worth getting up for to me. She opens the door with my head, pushing me in with her sensual teasing, now replaced with an impatient aggressive ram and a shove.

'How much can you drink for fuck sake?' she says, and I think the same about her whilst realising, of course, she hasn't actually touched a drop. There's a big bear of a man waiting inside the room, and someone smaller, more my size in a grey shirt and trench coat. This one's more dangerous in the way he's looking at me—that much I could tell from my past life. He means business; life, death or worse. I know that because that was my life before this one.

'What took you so long?' Trench Coat says, glaring at her.

'He can drink. He is meant to be Irish, after all,' she says, and as she does I instantly sense a mistaken identity even with this, my drunken brain.

'So, Sean, let's cut to it, no chitchat—where's Cherry?' And I'm picked up by the Bear and dumped onto a wooden chair in the centre of the room.

'Sean…Sean…the Bastard,' I mumble, starting to drool a little.

'Your parentage is of little concern. Where is she, fucker? Before this guy here starts ripping your fucking limbs off, then force feeds them back to you.'

The trench coat spits the words at me with genuine venom and I just shrug them, nonchalantly, back at him. They were serious and were the real deal here, but then again so was I. I'd seen this before on both sides of the fence and knew how it could go, plastered with liquor or not. The Bear takes three steps towards me whilst pulling his arm back, his hand forming a massive clenched fist which he then fires like a comet at the bridge of my nose. I pass out.

When I eventually come to, I see the room through blurred eyes and they're all stood immediately in front of me about a foot's length away—half a foot if you're bear-sized. My hands are bound behind me, around the chair, by the unmistakeable stickiness of carpet tape which pulls at the hairs on my hands and wrist. I'd been here before too.

Trench Coat, the devil's own bitch and the Bear are stood there; judge, jury and punishment or reward—I hadn't quite decided with her yet. The girl is waving a bottle of poppers in her hand that have been pushed under my nose to wake me, which stings like hell, and the chemicals make my chest pound like bass drums in my ears.

I notice my trousers and pants are round my ankles and I can now see the Bear is holding the handles of some bolt-croppers. I follow his clenched hands with my eyes down the shaft and to where the blades are poised, like a hand on a guillotine, around my cock and balls. From this I know they don't mean to mess around and they want an answer straight away. Trench Coat stares at me and moves towards my face, whispering...

'We asked you where she is, you don't answer. So now I need to make sure you don't put it in my girl ever again,' and he looks slowly at the Bear, who's only a breath away himself. The Bear's cold face tells me he isn't taking any pleasure, feeling or any disgust in this—he's a stone-cold soul.

'I'm not...Seannnn,' I just about get out, but I'm not sure if I do in time, or even if they're listening.

'Too late,' Trench Coat whispers in my ear, blowing me a kiss, and the Bear slowly moves his hands together. I look down to see a spurt of blood and black out for the second time.

I wake to an argument which seems to be about identity. They have my Moleskine notebook, coat, wallet, the envelope and the notes from a mystery postman or woman that got me into this, on the floor in front of them. I look down to see everything intact. They've nipped me enough to cause a shock that's for sure, and it's a bloody butcher's nick—but all intact. That would be the first and last time I literally put my balls on the line with my new life—or so I thought for now.

'Who the hell is this guy?' Trench Coat says to the girl. 'You only had one simple job—to pussy-draw the idiot in here. We couldn't wait for him to just drink himself to shit downstairs!'

'Didn't think he sounded very Irish… I don't know, how was I supposed to know? He asked for Cherry when he checked in. He's meant to be here isn't he? That's what he said!' she hits back.

'Not very Irish? No shit. Fuck me, girl. Look, this notebook is like a diary—sounds like we're in it and we hadn't even met him when he had it last!' And he kicks the notebook across the floor, still looking at her.

'He's a snooper, that's all, an inventive mind. Unlucky coincidence that he guessed right so far, that's all. Probably just a patsy Sean's sent across to take the fall.'

'Maybe,' Trench Coat says, looking me up and down. 'Cover that shit up, man, for fuck sake!'

The adrenaline, poppers, smack in the face and fear of losing my cock and balls has sobered me up a bit and the girl comes over to pull up my trousers and pants. Her head gets a bit close to it all down there as she kneels down looking at me in the eye, and in some ways it's worse torture than before. Although it does cross my mind, I wouldn't want to risk an erection in my current state; I might end up red-washing the room like a paint bomb.

'So, let's start over,' Trench Coat says, kicking the envelope, my notebook and the letters to my feet. 'What's the story behind all this shit? It's not in your little white notebook,' Trench Coat says, toeing it with his shoe on the floor.

'I'm not sure, it's taking shape though. You not figured it out yet, or do you want to prune my grapes some more?' I jest with ironically sized balls given the situation.

'Don't tempt us. If we don't get what we want out of this we might as well!' An empty threat, I'm sure, and I sense the tide has turned and they all know it. There's a switch of power as they don't know what side I'm on, and for all they know it could be theirs. I'm starting to suspect that is the case, as I look out at the morning sun beginning to come in and consider my next move.

'Stay with us, sonny, Jack, Bob or whoever the fuck!' And he looks at the Bear with one of those 'smack him into next century' looks, and the words snap me back into the room like a bullwhip.

'Alright, untie me first though, eh?' I say, looking back at my hands, attempting to look and sound as submissive as possible which halts the Bear's run up to attack. 'You've half drowned me in shitty cocktails, broken my face, poppered me up like I'm on Canal Street and my dick's half hanging off. I'm not up for any funny business!' They could tell from my look I was serious, but also not really weakened.

'Canal Street? Manchester eh?' he ponders, and I realise a shadow image of my past life has been let out.

'I've been there—who hasn't? It's the nineties. Everyone's spent a thought, dropped a pill or more from there.' My words make a connection—a kindred spirit maybe? Either that or a realisation I was useless and could die not giving anything away; or worse to them, I could have torn through my bonds at anytime and reaped havoc so it was pointless binding me up.

I was tired, but not enough for my eyes not to give something of the possibilities of a true self away. The girl, who's been kneeling in front of me having pulled up my trousers, opens my shirt and stands up. They all stand back and take a look; the Bear and the girl do one step each, but Trench Coat just does it in his mind and I see it in his eyes: a connection; a peer and an understanding. I've locked my past life away in a box in my head and hidden it in a cupboard along a lost corridor in my mind. A trick my mother told me when I was young, when my father left.

He was in the same cupboard—different box, but same cupboard. They might as well be taken aback by a Francis Bacon painting in all its bloody butchered glory—it's not me—I've disconnected from my past for now, but like any animal I'll use it if I have a mind to, if I'm cornered, prodded too much.

'Been through the mill before? Untie this guy before he unties himself.' Trench Coat gestures to the girl and turns his back to me in submission, whilst whispering something to the Bear who nods back in agreement. The girl kneels back down behind me this time, ripping the carpet tape off and whispering, 'I like the tough ones. Who dares wins,' then blowing a kiss by my ear.

'How about a drink?' I say, standing up slowly and brushing myself down before doing up my shirt. She laughs, thinking I'm joking, and the Bear also looks confused in disbelief but Trench Coat is already moving towards the mini bar—likeminded and more in common than I'd thought.

'Okay, let's try this a different way, friend,' he says, his words of sarcasm stinking out the room, along with the sweat of a hard night's work (on their part anyway). I just needed a shower.

In poker it would be three against one with me holding all the cards but them still not knowing if I was bluffing or not. What they have seen through the night and under my shirt though is that I'd played a harder game before, and was still here and without fear. So from their point of view, why risk it until they had a sense of what side I was on—or they best just get on with it and kill, or be killed.

Room service is ordered to go with the drinks and, despite his size, the Bear isn't eating.

'What does he run on?' I jest, as I finish my hair of the dog Scotch.

'Don't get funny,' Trench Coat jumps in before the other

two get a chance to react with me or against me. 'I think we might be in a similar boat together, but we aren't pals and this isn't a—'

'Who cares. You want Cherry don't you?' And I jump straight back in, taking the moment from him, adjusting the control of the situation. 'You're not the only ones—she's quite in demand. How did you pin me down as anything to do with it as soon as I arrived I wonder? This was all set up before I became part of it a day ago. The receptionist, the barman, your little act,' I go on, looking at her. 'This has all been planned or going for a while. What you didn't plan on was me popping up in the middle of it. Who's to say I'm not working for Cherry, or related? You could have just cut Cherry's brother's fucking dick off for fuck's sake!' I test them and they sign up for it, giving themselves away...

'She doesn't have a brother. And if she did he'd be a fuck sight better looking than you!' she says, with a hint of distant flirtation and a bit of last night's dance in her eyes. And so I get from this they know her well enough to know if she's got brother or not, so now I push it on a little further...

'She's not all that either,' I test, looking for a give-away signal. And then it comes: Trench Coat stiffens up straight away and his cards fall out in front of me showing his full hand.

'Shut it, fucker!'

'Oh, I get it. Why would you want to cut my junk off, whilst thinking I'm Sean? So I don't put it there again?' I look Trench Coat straight in the eyes. 'Been going on long, has it? Does Sean know? Bet he'd be quite made up with that, want to give you a gift or something, send you some flowers or worse, maybe even me. If he doesn't beat the shit out of her first!'

'You're sharp for a drunk waster.' The Bear speaks and it's surprisingly high-pitched, not as threatening as he looks at all and I can tell immediately why he's stayed quiet up until now; he's like a little girl on helium. I laugh a little but the others don't, and I look over at him as he rolls down his collar, revealing some sort of operation that's left him with a blow hole above where his Adam's apple should be.

'You should've gone for the lights. Them there cowboy killers, well they'll kill ya!' I say in a bad American accent and look at the Marlboro reds on the side table and then back at him. The Bear smacks me again and this time without the run up and I'm left flat out on the bed. I had asked for it this time, maybe I always had done. This time I expected it and I took it; after all it had been a long night and I needed the down time.

When I wake, I pretend I haven't, surveying the room through the slits of my eyes and with my ears also scanning the space. I can't hear any talking. The girl is alone on a chair pulled up to the side table, now in front of the window. She's looking out at the morning sun over a pile of my stuff and a black holdall which must be theirs.

One of her hands is under the table and I can't tell if she's scratching her leg or bored and playing with herself. I slowly stand and try not to make a sound, but she does though, moaning—she *is* playing with herself. The bed lets out a slight gasp of air from the mattress like an old cat fart, but it looks like she's too caught up in herself to notice.

I pick up the vase off the bedside table and edge my way towards her, cold, calculated and considered. I know just where to strike it over her head to knock her out, minimising the chance of any lasting damage. I time the strike with what I think is her starting to climax and she slumps into the seat then slides under the table, still murmuring in pleasure.

'Sweet dreams,' I mutter and wipe the blood, sweat and tears from my eyes.

I pick up my stuff from the table, take the holdall which seems half full of clothes and empty the mini bar on top. I put on my own black trench coat and leave the room, turning right towards the back stairs rather than taking the escalator or stairs to the lobby.

The stairs stink of cigarettes and my cock hurts from the minor snip of last night. The fact the bag I'm carrying has spare clothes that look more Trench Coat's cut than hers or the Bear's means he was probably going to do the rest of any messy work required. My downstairs hurts and stings where the formation of a scab is pulled off by the rubbing of my trouser zip as I walk. I decide I need to strap it up, as I pass a first aid box on the wall in the stairwell. I open it and take out a bundle of plasters, rip them open one at a time with my mouth and a spare hand, as the other drops my trousers and pants to the floor. I stretch my parts up like I'm strangling a turkey, plastering it to the bottom of my stomach best I can, trying to close the wound on the top of it. As I look up an old lady is staring in horror at me, mouth open, and the fag she was smoking seems to drop from her mouth in slow motion to the concrete step below her, as sparks bounce and fly from it.

'What the...?' she tries to get out but is too shocked.

'Fuck. What the fuck!' I finish for her. 'Literally a hard one, madam. In fact ,it damn nearly ripped it clear off!' And I motion with my hands at it.

'I, ahem, I...' Her words are still stuck in her throat, with her mouth wide and the previous draw on the fag slowly moving out of her body like a Highland fog.

'Move along, dear, nothing more to see here,' I say, pulling everything back up and doing up my belt. I pick up her dropped cigarette as I pass, take a drag and offer it back to her. 'Have a nice day,' I smile.

She doesn't take it, mouth still gasping. And I shrug, moving further down the staircase with a little bit more spring in my step. I want to get to the car before she raises any sort of alarm and because my knob doesn't feel quite as much like it's being sawn off by my zip any more.

I leave through a side door, setting off an alarm as I push the bar to open it, and step out into the bright light of the morning. I'm sure the alarm will freeze people on the spot for about ten seconds before they actually realise what it is, all the staff included. Then again, the staff will have to recall their training and procedure in the event of a fire, by which time I'll be gone from here. Trench Coat, the Bear and the girl can scramble round in that big corporate punch bowl as much as they like, having lost me to the Welsh air and what might be their contact to Cherry, who seems to be Trench Coat's squeeze and also Sean's girl.

They needed me more than I needed them, although I did want the girl that worked with them but that was off-piste, and what I want and need are different today. I will have forgotten wanting her in a day or two but they'll still need answers. Besides, judging by her little act in the room before I left, the chances are she's more into herself than me.

14

I walk straight to the car and don't look back, stubbing out the cigarette on a BMW's roof on the way past, before opening the door of the Saab then throwing in the bag and myself. I can't pause for respite, not now. I need sea air to reset myself and so drive straight off, heading south-west on the M4 towards Bridgend. I always need sea air at some point or another; must be the Viking in me. Same blood that would give me Dupuytren's disease later in life, like my grandfather, and no doubt it would twist my hand like a witch's claw, as the tendons got amassed with sinew until a surgeon would slice it open to relieve the pressure, just like his.

My past life was rearing its head again, and yet again with a mere word from a stranger touching upon it, in a mention of Manchester. As the girl had opened my shirt, she had sent my mind down into the corridor I'd created in my head. With each button she pulled at, I'd got nearer and nearer to that hidden mental cupboard and as the shirt opened, the contents of the lost box and my previous life was spilled back out in front of me, guts and all, to see again.

So, I decided I would head for the sea and put old demons to bed forever, letting this new person I'd invented breathe. The PI in me was trying to get out and do something that might make some sense, redeem my soul or keep some kind of sanity. The identity that I'd formed needed to indulge my natural urges, rather than locking me in and suppressing me in a job, like in the witness protection programme the police had straitjacketed me in.

I'd have to decide and move on before I could get back to the case. They were on ice here, they weren't going anywhere. This way, after the beach and sea, I'd return back and on form and with the case thought through. A private mended dick and sleuthhound with no distractions from my other self or selves. I'd keep the strengths, and box up and burn the rest...

The road opens up ahead of me and again I'm tempted to just drive on, not stop and just keeping going and stay in whatever B&B, hotels and holes would take me and my fake fifties. As I drift on into oblivion, the draw of the sea is more overwhelming than any gypsy whim (also in my blood) and so I keep on the M4 past St Mellons and Coychurch then dogleg with the road at Bridgend aiming for the sea, sand and my destiny.

Forty minutes later and I am breaking free of the motorway and onto the small little country roads that typify the best of Britain's rural veins and I can see in the distance the land ending as the horizon becomes a comforting blurred line between sky and sea.

I reach over to the open holdall on the passenger seat, moving the black shirt and jeans to one side to reveal the black carpet tape used to bind me earlier and a tightly wrapped white brick of cocaine in polythene. Another piece of the jigsaw reveals itself and drops into place, as does the realisation Sean knew about Cherry's affair, which was the argument I heard the other day.

He must have kept her from going to meet Trench Coat on her usual drugs mule run and sent me there instead, like a lamb to the slaughter. He must have told them he was coming across to sort it out himself—so they were all waiting for me, thinking I was him, with guns blazing and knives sharpened!

Yes, just go across there, John, like a mug, meet Cherry's lover, give him a couple of grand in fake fifties to seal the deal. I turn up to take it on the chin and worse, with blades around my cock and balls. So, Cherry's missing, Sean's in on it and wants his drugs to keep people off his back in Bristol. They are most likely connected to the feisty characters in the Star & Garter that tried to scare me, which was better than being neutered by Trench Coat who wants his money, drugs and the girl.

It was a mess and I loved it, but there was something I had to do now. I couldn't have any more ghosts from the past. I needed to take the strengths and bury everything else at sea. If I couldn't, then it would be the end of me and if I'm not in control of my life, I'll head out into the sea myself, and be in control of my death instead.

I drive down through winding lanes, privet hedges high on either side, the roads fading from tarmac two cars wide to shades of mud one car wide. I pass a pub on the right of the road in a small hamlet called Monknash and I take a mental note. A pint in the fresh air would do me good at some point, as would breaking up a fake fifty, but I keep myself from distraction and push the car on down the dirt track to the end, passing a farm.

It looks like it's leading me and the car into a river or stream but it doesn't and stops as the road splits in two. There are even smaller tracks, both gated off; the left has an old wooden stile with a footpath through the trees to the sea, rocks, sand and what would be the resting place for my sins of yesterday—that or all of me.

I pull the car onto the grass and take the holdall and place all my pieces on top. My white Moleskine notebook, notes that arrived through the door and envelope are all part of the same story now—it's too late for me to get out of this situation and separate myself.

Like the roads I'd driven on, the path I walk down slowly transforms from dirt track a tractor wide to a pebbled path a person wide, with the trees that arch overhead dissipating to open skies and I'm greeted by the entrance to what feels like a bay or cove. Two grassy hills frame the track which winds down the middle of them to the giant stone flats—cliffs formed where the hills were halted by the sea, and rock pools with a band of sand beneath go on as far as I can see.

The rocky cliffs' layers are exposed, showing time, the past and all its dirt for the sea to cleanse and wash away and I know I'm in the right place. I stare out to sea, walk ten paces like a dead man on the green mile, drop the bag by a rock and sit on its smooth cold top as the sea air and an occasional drop of the waves hits my face.

An hour passes and an eerie sea fret has descended around me, touching the water's surface, which appears as black as blood in moonlight. I walk to the water's edge and pick up smooth flat stones. I examine them and discard them when I find a better one, until I have three palm-sized, almost perfectly round stones. Then I return to my post and sit holding the rocks in my hands, looking into the misty distance. It stirs my heritage and my blood as I look through the mist and sea fret to see a Viking longboat emerging and approaching silently with a lone warrior on board.

Before it reaches shore the lone warrior stands slowly and I see his strength and fortitude. I stand, take off my jacket, slowly unbutton and drop my shirt, exposing my flesh like it's my true self, an armour, as the crisp cold air wisps around my scarred torso where knives, flames and shrapnel have all played a part. My SAS service tattoo (a reminder to myself from '94) looks an inky blue in the light and mist as the early evening creeps all around the beach. I stoop slowly down, looking my Viking in the face, pick up the three stones I'd carefully selected and I walk to the water's edge, each step an eternity, stopping at my alter-ego.

We stand face to face, with stony unflinching expressions, a mirrored self and force of the ages. I select my first stone and draw my arm back to skim it out to sea, into the mist, and as I do, my counterpart fades out into the sea with it.

15

As the first stone leaves my hands and before it hits the waves, it opens a window to the past in my mind and I see it all before me; what got me into this, all the memories. I can see the start of me and the strength I'd built and then John Barrie, my assigned ID given to me by the authorities which I've re-made into this mess I am now…

The first stone's memories are of when my mother used to work in a pub, whilst I was locked upstairs with a black-and-white TV. I heard all the drinking, brawling and cheering. I could smell it, feel it, and it seeped into the very core of my being before I'd even touched a drop myself.

She'd taken to locking me upstairs, above the pub, as her previous tactic of letting me run free on the streets resulted in me breaking into garages, offices and industrial units for amusement. Things came to a head one day when CCTV footage emerged in a local newspaper of a small child taking a shit in the paper tidy on the desk of a local businessman. You couldn't see the face but she knew it was me and so I was locked upstairs, out of sight and out of mind.

So, like recently when restrained and shackled by an office job, I went out of my mind. My imagination and independence soared within the old plastic casing of the black-and-white TV; I was everywhere and nowhere.

When I became old enough to get sent away to school, I was, and ejected even further out of sight and mind to the other side of the county and it was a big county. Whilst a barmaid's wages couldn't buy you private schooling, it could however, together with single parent credentials, get you access to a seven-day state school boarding system which amounted to an old school borstal and with it all the extra training for me which inevitably flowed from the fellow inmates there.

I'd passed my first round of training on the streets and in the pub moving onto the next level. At school after the fourth or fifth beating—caned and hit for some innocuous act or behaviour, deemed unworthy by them—I was toughened up as much as a child of that age should ever be.

The teachers at the school were shipped in from even more evil schools on the Scottish borders that had been closed but which had all been old converted military camps and shelters. Here the teachers were the law and they enforced their will on the children with an iron fist, which often held a ruler, bar, shoe, cane or whatever was close to hand. The kids, a lot of them from harder situations at home, all lapped it up, associating the pain and beatings with some connection to home, a parent or a show of respect amongst peers in a gang as they compared strap marks and bruises; badges of honour. I'd been hit for sleep walking and woke up mid-trike as it hit my young flesh. I didn't make a single sound—stared ahead, took it.

Days later, before the bruises had faded and gone, I would find my best friend hanging by his own belt in my locker. Life was hard, but I had learnt to be harder. Nothing easy is worth fighting for, getting up for or taking your first few steps in the morning for—you need a destination.

It was only after leaving school that I was told corporal punishment was banned before I'd even arrived there, and a lot of the behaviour and excessive force by the teaching staff was a rebellion against a system they had no control over. The children's scars, inside and out, eventually became a lasting legacy and by-product of the staff's bitterness, of an archaic dying method and their backwards mindsets.

And I learnt another lesson: people will use other people for their own means and whether you're a pawn, king or queen it doesn't matter unless you're the hand that moves it all on the board.

Towards the end of school, aged sixteen, I filled out a questionnaire with the rest of my year and a careers advisor to see what to do with my life next and after they decided we waited as a long line of lost teens to get given our futures.

One of the kids came out of the room having been given his occupation by a questionnaire and the teachers bark from in there, 'Farmer!' Another got given 'truck driver', another one 'teacher'. I didn't feel too optimistic and I decided before the test that I wanted to be an artist, a painter, writer or sculptor—just anything to be alone. Like my escape through the old black-and-white TV in the pub, I wanted to be alone in an imagined world.

I thought I'd rig my answers in the questionnaire to suit and try to control the outcome. The basic and remedial questionnaire had limited output options though, and so pigeonholed us into any variety of fields with a narrow view of the world that could only come from a form written to force children into one of five professions to support a local rural community—heaven help them if any ever had aspirations beyond the village fields and walls.

Any answer from the child suggesting a degree or desire towards creativity immediately pigeonholed them, and so I was. Even the teacher was embarrassed to read it out, but she eventually spat it out at me after some period of staring: 'You're going to be a flower arranger.' I ignored it and it would form part of a big heap of ignored bureaucracy in my life. Another lesson was learnt: do what you want with your own options, just create those options yourself.

I left school, joined the army and every face or target I saw down a barrel became one of those teachers that raised a hand, turned a blind eye to the abuse, and ignored my friend as he turned blue, tongue out, strangled, dying in my locker.

I pushed on for more training and strength, shaping my intellect alongside, all of which would be useful in what I needed now if I was to survive. The first stone finishes skimming on over the water; thirteen bounces and then a small twist and a turn as it drifts down in sideways jolt, side to side to the sea bed.

I pick up the second stone which feels flat and shiny, clenching it for a while with my knuckles turning white to the bone, and then I cast it out into the mist. As I do, the next chapter from the hidden recesses of my mind opens up to me. I see the army training; mud, sweat and pain. At that time, in the past, the sun probably shone but in my head it was all rain in my face, blisters and bruised collar bones from the repetitive rifle recoils on the Otterburn ranges.

Border Reivers had hardened the region for hundreds of years and now the hardest, most resilient fusilier regiments resided there—or so we were programmed to think. Be tough, let the history of the hills be your training, and take over the shell of your body as you spit and vomit your way through it all. Be more, be the best—bollocks. A dose in Bosnia for the UN, wearing a blue helmet as each side took random shots at us as target practice, formed the many scars, both emotional and physical, that were to stay with me forever. Still, I pushed on to find myself and my limit.

The moon, reflecting off the black of the flat sea, glares at my eyes and, for a moment, I'm taken back to a time a tank next in line in my convoy was blown up in front of me. The horror, flames and the blast builds up and fades, subsiding in my vision and I'm back at the shore again and left with the glow of the moon, the screams and flames now a distant subconscious murmur of ghosts rattling around in my skull.

The second stone is halfway through its skimming across the water. Time has slowed down and I'm on into the next flow of my memories. After the army grew too familiar to me and easy on my bones, I craved more and more, all with a degree of autonomy that I wasn't going to experience in that unit. So, I applied for SAS selection and endured another level of being pushed way beyond what I believed possible in myself and the human condition.

The real test came to me some years after the pain of actual service and training had subsided. The memories of my service, which included Northern Ireland, moved around in my head, continuing to wake me in the night like the echoes of the machine guns in my ears. What I'd seen, done, felt and witnessed was all unforgiveable to me. I couldn't get a grasp on the reason why, and the 'Ours is not to question why, but to do or die.'

It just didn't stick when I was expected to be killing my fellow men on home ground. An episode by a town hall in Ireland, where we lay in wait to ambush a massively outnumbered and out-trained handful of men who had staged a demonstration of sorts with a mounted machine gun on the back of a lorry, left me shaken to the core of my very being.

Their bullets hit walls sending shrapnel into my chest and arms—I still aimed, but wouldn't fire back. They shot up the dust and soil in front of me—still I wouldn't fire. I'll kill for me, you and your children or in the name of self-preservation—not for a god or politics though, never. My fellow soldiers cut them down and I was discharged, and despite the nightmares to follow that would wake me in the night, I felt better for it.

I already have the third stone in my hand as the second finishes skipping seventeen times, stopping dead and dropping to the sea bed.

The mist has cleared overhead and I look up at the stars, the infinity of space. A scream leaves my mouth, primal and guttural. I return my gaze to the sea, looking out and again drawing my arm back and then forcing it out into the darkness, more forceful than the previous two and ferocious in the knowledge I'm nearly done and will have to face what comes after.

The third stone in my hand was my last chapter to bury and the one that held the story that stole my identity. This one would see my insides turned out, food for the fish to bloat up on as I give my real self a chance at a fresh start. The sea would take it all for me and bury it together forever.

I throw it and the stone speeds on, and on, making first contact with the surface of the water I see it: the bright lights and strobes of it all, the drugs, gangs, guns and sheer rawness of it all that came next, to put me under witness protection.

If you catch the ferry from Dublin to Holyhead you hit a different type of war zone in the north-west of England. I passed through Liverpool and followed the beat of the drums that was mid-90s Manchester. It was like flowers to a bee, or open legs to a serviceman that had been without for some time, and I had been without for such a long time.

I devoured it in handfuls and I didn't have to introduce

myself before fellow ex-servicemen, including me, had all gravitated together and I was put to use on the door of a number of nightclubs. I was passed around like a rabid dog to keep the right sort of rough with money inside the clubs, whilst keeping the wrong sort of rough, the ones selling drugs that weren't pushed by my employers, out of the club.

There was trouble: knives, guns waved in the air and shots fired into bar fronts and windows, women distracted whilst men tried to push in and it was all the next level in my repertoire and ammunition to put to use later—now, on this case, if I can see it through.

The bands that played in the clubs were as bad as the door staff and punters, and from the front line of the Hacienda I saw all I could want to see, and a lot of things I wish I hadn't. The guy running it all (unnamed) was like Fagin from Oliver Twist—a shadowy spectre, creeping through the streets below the railway arches opposite the club entrance, directing teens, mere children, to carry out his will and orchestrating the security staff to make sure each night went as planned.

Bands and DJs played, people gathered in hordes and masses at the church of plenty, with pills, powder and smokes all distributed down through the approved channels like veins to the wanting, needy and addicted. Anyone trying to get into the club to sell a little for themselves, or a rival gang attempting to pollute the supply, was dealt with using the same brutality and indiscrimination; a warning to those gangs to keep to their own back yard, and to amateurs to leave it to the big boys.

Knees were capped, flesh cut and extra scars earned on my own skin. The Hacienda was built on such things, all despite the misconception it was anything to do with a record label, so why not defend its cash flow, I thought, as it was also my own—particularly as it paid my way and honed my skills even further.

We were all puppets of someone in a self-perpetuating circle of pollutants, violence and hedonistic escapism.

On Friday 14th June 1996, after a few years earning my stripes and respect on the doors, something happened, and my life would never be my own again. Not as I knew it. My identity would be taken from me and I'd be left forever reinventing myself to act out whatever I needed to survive and just get by from then on. Eventually what happened was that I'd had enough; the immorality of being asked to face and fight fellow men in Ireland for religion and political borders was one thing, but to do it to feed a hedonistic monster that lined evil pockets, tainting my own in the process, was another type of dirty war and I'd dived into it, swallowed deep, choked on and was ready to get out of.

We justified our presence, and soothed our consciences with the understanding that we were keeping the flow of product pure, a good clean night to be had by all, while all inside happily parted with their hard-earned cash, student loans and the contents of pockets picked from the streets.

But, when a young girl took something, mixed the wrong thing or overdosed, toppling from the stage, one leg staying on the stage as the other hit the floor two or three foot below her, a spray of blood shot up the front of her little white dress and as she passed out in my arms, fading out of the world, something in me was born, as another part of me died from that world.

As I carried her from the club through the smoky crowd, past the fellow security personnel and dancers, all of them turned a blind eye to favour their own good times, continuing to dance, deal and die, all of them. Their souls sold for their ignorance. My resolve was made even stronger and so I stood up against them all, the evil, the ignorant and the shameful spectre himself, as I named each one of them in court and as I did so, I erased anything of myself. Having been through it and played my part as a cog in the machine, I wouldn't be myself anymore—and I didn't want that anyway.

On that Saturday morning in Manchester—the one after the night that would change me and my identity forever by standing up in court against my peers—at 9.20am, a white Ford cargo truck pulled up by a post box on Corporation Street, parking outside Marks & Spencer and below the bridge across from the Arndale Centre. Two hooded men left the truck and walked calmly away whilst 80,000 shoppers, workers, street cleaners and hung-over revellers packed into the streets to go about their weekend. Granada TV studios received the first warning, with a recognised code word, and then the local radio stations and papers took the same call.

The IRA shook the city, but drugs and gangs had already ripped it apart years earlier and would continue to do so long after the city centre was rebuilt. 1500kg of IRA Semtex couldn't drown out the shotguns of Moss Side or the bass line to 'Blue Monday'. Mannequins were blasted from shop windows, buildings felled and traffic stopped dead, but the people stood firm like the concrete casts of Pompeii. The bomb blast whistled and roared around them, but unlike Pompeii, these people, in this city, were already made of stone.

The last skimming stone stops. I stare out into the sea for a while then return to the bag and take out the roll of carpet tape that was used to bind me in the hotel. I undo my fly and grab the turkey's neck once more, remove the now damp, stained plasters and tape myself up and then do up my trousers. I had dumped my memories out to sea, and now I would reset myself. I would swim out into the sea, at least as far as the furthest stone had gone. In fact, I'd swim as far as I could without stopping and until I ached, muscles seizing up and I couldn't swim anymore, and with the icy cold waters lapping at my body and purging my mind—I'd let the oceans dissolve away my past. And then when I couldn't go out any further I'd turn back and aim for shore, with a new identity born or one that couldn't live and would instead rest at sea.

If I could summon up the strength of self-preservation I would deserve it and be reborn into this, from the seas where my ancestors came and landed before me. As I stare out across the water, my Viking alter-ego stands on the bow of his boat, about as far out as I could possibly hope to get—he's inviting me to join him, in death or in life; the spirit of my past and ancestors are there waiting for me and I'll use that spirit in life or death, for good—forever.

I dive in with the icy cold waters all around me and it drips off the stubble on my chin and I power on into the night like a machine. I swim, leaving the shore and my past behind me.

16

I pull my body through the icy, silver water and it gets heavier and heavier, draining my arms and legs of all energy. My breath gasps and wheezes out in front of me, each stroke weighing more and more as though I'm swinging giant dumbbells through freezing treacle.

A storm closes in and crashes around me as I hit my first wall of endurance and stop still, except for my legs treading under the surface. My chest beats and pounds away in pain, echoing in my ears as pellets of rain crash onto my naked shoulders and tear into the sea like a hail of bullets all around me. My eyes sting with the torrent from above and I slowly close them then force myself on with the muscle memory of past challenges that I've faced and finished—I'd been through a wall or two of pain before in my life, pushing through to the other side, emerging a stronger beast of a man and I would again now. In recent months, I'd lost it, the verve I once had, but now I would give it a chance to return and fill me; nature's gift—and the monster inside.

By the time the second wall of pain hits me, my body's past and recent events have taken their toll. I come to a stop a few feet away from my imagined counterpart, the Viking, and as I'm only just able to summon the strength to tread water, he reaches out to me over the edge of his boat and I push on to meet him.

He lies down on the deck of his boat with his head over the edge then leans forward over just enough so we're eye to eye. We stare at each other for what feels like an eternity until I raise my arms, shut my eyes, and sink slowly through the infinite blackness of the icy water; my feet are then caressed by the sand as I hit the sea floor in a cloud of silt.

A crash of lighting over the sea's surface, which is about ten feet overhead, lights up an area around me and I open my eyes again. A second crack and a bang lights me up again, deep in the water, and he's there in front of me. The warrior of my past. His hair drifts around wildly like an angry octopus as he starts to scream, a battle cry, and I follow his lead.

A relentless fury fills the sea with the bubbles from our cries absorbed silently into the waters around us. The sea takes all in, in a wave, like it's taking a deep breath, then forces itself back at us with the strength and spirit of all time pushing me back up to the water's surface alone and I aim for shore, exhausted and drained, uncertain if I'll make it, but knowing if I do it will be for my future self to be reborn, or I'll sink again with my weakened self laid here to rest with the Viking of my past.

17

As I lie on the shore, face down, my fingers feel the grains of sand underneath. Slowly clawing out, rubbing them between fingertips to examine them, the texture, the land I'd returned to, and then I let them fall. I pass out, head in hands and hands in the sand.

Opening my eyes slowly to the night, I'm on my back and can see into a vast blanket of stars above me. I sense another presence and warmth and roll onto my side to see a spaniel looking at me, with its nose an inch from my face. I blink slowly, and it's still there when I open my eyes, and then it gives my face a single lick in sympathy, as if to say hello. Its sad, friendly face says it all. I feel a fire's heat and see another body silhouetted and dancing in its flickering light in front of me.

'Mercy, mercy me.'

Softly spoken words from the silhouetted character caress me with the warmth of the fire, sounding like those of an old granddad picking up his granddaughter out of a nettle patch. The safety of the words and the heat smother my tested frame in something I haven't felt in a long time and I pass out again into a deep rest, touched by the caring sentiment of one stranger to another.

I wake and look up, expecting to see a camp thespian for some reason, but instead I see a hardened old country gent, more like a Connery Bond—a world of stories, incident and strength in his face. His eyes are windows into experiences maybe similar to mine but with more years and notches on the post to show for it.

He's sat on a rock opposite me huddled over a fire which he's crafted, complete with tins hanging from it. I can smell the strong rich stench of coffee. The spaniel notices I've woken up before he does, or it acknowledges it first, with a kind dog smile, a pant of excitement and a tail wag.

'Back with us, are we, in the land of the living?' he says, gazing into the fire, and he prods the embers, making them dance for us; a warming dance of mini red dresses in the cold chill of the night. I say nothing and look back through the flames waiting for my brain to catch up with reality. And it does. Slowly but surely, synapses fire up and defrost along with my skin and hands.

'Don't know what you were playing at. Lucky I happened by. What were you swimming away from, or to?'

'The past,' I say.

'You won't escape it out there, not in that chilly kelp soup.'

'I've washed enough off to move on, kept what I need to get by.'

'I hope you didn't swallow any.'

'It swallowed me, whole, spat me out.'

'A few demons eh?' His grave voice sounds like he's been there himself before.

'Maybe… but some of them I've kept for good measure—to face a demon or two if I need to.'

'We've all got ghosts, sonny, don't need to near kill ourselves to face them—they're with us from birth, forevermore.'

'I'm back, I've survived—and I'm stronger for it.' I grin through the flames at him, as I recognise an ex-military demeanour, and he does so in me. We look at each other for a while. A serious look and we can feel the stories passing between us in the night tossed around in the fire's light. Even the dog has adopted a respectful, sombre posture and looks on at her master, and occasionally looks back at me with the same look.

'Which was it, Ireland?' He refers to service, probably coming from his own experience and seeing it in me.

'Amongst others—it was the one that broke me though.'

'Ugly isn't it, killing brothers for a religion and country you don't understand. Not like defending a school or rescuing a wife and child from a fire is it? You ignore their religion, politics and save them because they're human. Not ignore it and shoot to kill like all that shit over there.'

'We're all brutal tools of someone, something.' The word brutal hangs on my lips with the blood and scars delivered and received for other people's causes flashing before me in an instant.

'Doesn't look like you are anymore. Standing alone against something now, are you?'

'You got anything stronger than coffee?' I ask, wanting a real drink.

'Milk?' he says, smiling and holding up a half-bottle of Jameson Whiskey. I smile too and hold out my hand to receive a tin mug of coffee, which he tops up with a healthy measure. I notice I'm a wrapped in a tartan blanket up to the shoulders and it drops down to my waist as I reach out. I notice he's put me in one of the spare black shirts from Trench Coat's bag and I remember the drugs, fake notes, my notebook. I look around quickly and he reaches under his legs.

'Looking for this? It's all there. This stuff will kill you, you know!'

'The coke would, fake fifties might, notebook definitely will, eventually. I'm not finished with it yet,' I say, looking at the bag and wondering what his next move will be. After all, we'd shared a rapport, both servicemen together. How far or hard mine was, he doesn't know yet though. Do I come clean, spill it out? His nurse maid act could just be an interrogation technique, or worse, maybe he means to test to see if there's any more and when he finds out he means to move on without me and cash in.

'Stop it!' His words bark out at me, halting my analysis and pulling me back to the beach, fire, him and his dog. 'Just stop it. I can see you trying to figure out my angle. Am I a friend or foe, what do I want, where do I fit in with this mess you've got yourself into?'

He taps at my white notebook with his index finger, flicks to a random page in it and begins to read it out loud; my thoughts, mind and story about to be spilt onto the evening's beach, mixing together with the crabs, bottles and used condoms. Yesterday's filth and scabs. All of it.

'WAIT!' I stop him.

'Yeah, my counsellor or therapist had me writing something similar. It didn't stop the bombs ringing in my head waking me up each night, with the tremors and the screams of burning children.'

'Just wait,' I say again, softer this time. 'I think we need to change gear a little—and cheer the fuck up! Less coffee, more milk.' And I hold up my mug and nod my head at the bottle by his feet.

'Right you are, son. Yeah, you're right, let's start over.' He nods, picks up the bottle, topping us both up with a giant measure to calm our demons and lubricate the angels so we can talk freely again. I take a gulp, then a sip. He does this too and his dog chews on some mermaid's purses. One pops, sending salt water into the air. The dog pauses, looks at the droplets falling to the sand then continues to chew on balls of seaweed.

'Ali, stupid dog,' the man says, smiling and looking down.

'Ali?'

'After my wife.'

'I thought we were going to cheer up?'

'She's still alive, you cheeky bastard!' he says, chuckling to himself and I join in, looking back up at the sky which is still clear and full of stars, out to infinity.

'Won't she be wondering where you are, your wife?' I wonder out loud.

'She's probably halfway through throwing my pension away on a game of poker with her friends at the moment, back at the house. The sherry will all be finished too by the time I get back. She's used to me going off on walks at night, staying out a bit. Helps her sleep—me too, eventually. Stops the bombs for a bit, I guess.'

It seems his nights might be different to mine, albeit the end result is the same. With all the restlessness, bad dreams and a thirst you can't quench despite thinking it will help to pour a good dose on top. We're both chewed-up remnants of other people's pain, celebrated in our own discomforts.

'The plough seems to follow me all over, wherever I go,' I say, looking at the constellation above me, and changing the subject to higher things.

'Should have been a farmer,' he quips, still looking at his dog and chuckling away to himself and his wife-named spaniel, Ali the dog.

'Isn't it confusing having two things with the same name?'

'Two bitches, one name. Simple enough for even me to remember. They both do what they want and have me running round in circles for them anyway.'

'I'll not ask who's better in bed,' I say and he stops sniggering, looks at me with feigned anger then starts chuckling away to himself again, as he shakes his head slowly.

We consume food out of tins and it's hard to not feel like cowboys with the moon, fire, sand and the old timer. After the whiskey has loosened me up and the food has lined my innards we get back down to the hard talk: the mess, the case and the girls.

I may be a fool for opening up to a stranger but it feels like he'd saved my life, and is interested or just amused, one of the two, so I spill it back out on the sand in front of us, the whole truth and nothing but the truth. Except, that is, any more real facts to do with my identity or change of it; I am ex-military, now a private eye as far as he is concerned, and he laps it up like his dog did the stinking seaweed at our feet. 'That dog's going to sick or shit all that back up again, probably in the back of your car you know!' I state as if I know something about dogs.

I'd already told him the overview of the case as I saw it: the missing girl, who's having an affair, me being sent by her boyfriend to collect her with a bundle of fake cash in payment, me being beaten by dealers at the mention of his name on the way out of town and then turning up to the hotel like an idiot with the money to take another kicking as other people are waiting there expecting Sean with drugs to complete a deal. And they also want her, and really bad, as the guy she's having the affair with is there too, and seems to be running the whole show. I omit the bit where I nearly get turned into a eunuch, because I don't want to re-imagine it again and would rather forget it— the first and last time I'd put my balls on the line.

'Aye, she'll be sick most likely. She loves it but doesn't know when to stop before it makes her ill. Bit like you with drink and people,' he speaks with a subtle, south-westerly accent on the aye. 'So the case, has it got you beaten?'

'No, I'm back. Just need to get my head straight, understand the game that's being played and show my hand to the right side.'

'What makes you think I'm on the right side? Not in on the game too?' He speaks into the fire and his face looks serious as the shadows flicker over his nose and eyes. His tone has also shifted to being less playful and I wonder: in my training, I had taken the hard interrogation, then got the mop-you-up, motherly sort. One would break you then the other would patch you up and seek to get you to open up that way. I look at his face and can see it, a puppeteer and master at work. He's no soft, salty sea dog—ex-military, he said it himself—which then makes me think, like me, if that's what he would say about himself… there must be more. He moves his gaze slowly and seriously from the fire, fixing both eyes on me.

'I'll say it again, sonny, what makes you think I'm on side?'

'What makes you think I haven't considered it and told you what I wanted you to know?'

'Because when I found you, you were mumbling most of this shit anyway. By the time you'd defrosted in front of the fire, you just confirmed what I already knew, one way or another.'

As he taps my notebook three shadows, instantly recognisable, emerge from behind him and walk slowly towards us, with the sand and rocks barely making a sound.

'You can come over now,' he speaks, and they're already close.

'What was your signal to get them over when you were through with me?'

'Wasn't one, but the dog went to see them. Thought it best to come clean.' And I look over to see Ali, the dog at their feet smiling up at Trench Coat, the Bear and the girl.

'We've a little job of our own for you, soldier boy,' Trench Coat says.

'Easy, lad, we were just building up a rapport here, no need to get frosty! We all want the same thing,' the old man says, in control. He must be their governor.

'I'm not working with drug dealers—pound your own meat for all I care. Missing girl case, that's all it is to me,' I say.

'Sit down you three, you're scaring the fish,' the old man orders and they pick a rock each around the fire. The Bear sits opposite me, the girl and Trench Coat either side of the Governor. I see fit not to let slip that half of my motives behind wanting to find the girl is because she's hot, as Trench Coat's already expressed how much he hates someone playing his patch, and that was most, if not all, that created this whole mess in the first place. I go to stand up, and none of them move.

'Leave if you want, but I think you'll be interested.'

'I don't think so. Go to Bristol and get her yourself. There's four of you savage bastards. Five if you seriously account for him,' I say, looking over at the Bear. They all smirk, and the old guy picks up my white notebook and some letters from the top of the bag.

'You're forgetting something. What you haven't told me is in here. Makes quite a read you know. Some people in Manchester and Salford would pay well to get their hands on it, you'd imagine,' he says, tapping each word out with his index finger on the front cover as they hammer out the threat, the blackmail. 'Let's not fall out. You know where Sean is. He thinks you're working for him, just take the money and this powder and he'll open up to you. Find out where she is—we'll do the rest and take it, the money and everything off him. He means nothing to you. He's Sean the Bastard according to this.' And he taps again, throwing me a weighty stare for good measure.

'Find him and her too! And let us know where to do the pickup,' Trench Coat summarises.

'You've three days, then we're making a call to Manchester,' the Governor concludes. And I'm done up good, as far as they're concerned.

'If you open that all up you're a fool. We'll all die,' I threaten. 'They play tough.'

'How's the balls, soldier boy?' the girl teases and I feel them tighten.

'How's the head? Didn't interrupt you when I left last time did I?' And I steer the genital-based digs back at her, thinking of back in the hotel when I cracked her over her head when she was mid-wank.

'Stop flirting you two! Soldier boy, gangster, doorman or whatever—PI DRUNKEN FUCK, I don't care—you've three days!' Trench Coat says, losing patience, picking up the black bag, as the Governor holds out something that looks like a black brick.

I look closer, and it has a handset on it and is a first-generation mobile phone. A mobile if you had a wheelbarrow, and a phone if you were an 80s yuppie with a BMW and Chelsea pinstriped suit.

'What the fuck is that? Got anything smaller?'

'Three days, and we'll keep this shit,' he says, skimming some of the fakes off the top of the bag and zipping it up before throwing the bag to my feet. 'Take Sean his precious powder if it makes him give her up.'

And as the words leave his lips I have no doubt they intend to have everything in hand when I report her and his whereabouts back to them. Sean is a lone trader, I think, and out of his depth with this lot across the water in Wales who are after him now. The Star & Garter pub contingent obviously want their fill too. Throw Cherry into the mix and Trench Coat is going to have some new baubles on his tree this year; snip, snip, sack and all.

'There's only one number in that brick, so you can get us easily,' the Governor jumps in. 'Keep the little white book too, looks like you need it to cry your mind into. We have the name in Manchester to call if you disappear or double cross us. Pretty easy to remember isn't it? The case was in all the papers. Just don't stab us in the back too like you did them, or we'll feed you to them, or send your head up to them in a box as a present!' And the tough old granddad closes the night's meeting with this, the weight of his words and a cold stare.

As I walk up the beach I smile to myself and it must have looked evil if there was anyone to see it—I could feel it though, the power in me. They all think they have it all wrapped up and that they're in control. Both sides do, Sean and the motley crew on the shore here. They don't though, and before the old fella's dog throws up its next load of seaweed, I could call in some ex-colleagues and run them all down before they knew what had hit them, or I could take my time and take them myself one at a time. Or, not so much fun, but I could drop out and call the police, confess all and take a slap on the wrist.

Thing is though, the girl, Cherry. Where is she if she wasn't at the hotel with them? Did Sean send me off to complete his deal, knowing full well she wasn't coming back anyway? I had a case to sort, my first pair of shoes to wear in and I wanted to see that cherry-red hair again.

I stop halfway up the sand, drop the bag and blanket, then get out a black shirt and coat (also a trench coat), put them both on then walk on to the car. I don't look back at them, all four sat huddled around the fire behind me as the sun has started to rise and my shadow creeps forward, growing out in front of me.

I went into the sea torn, tattered, and a shadow of my past and present. I'm different now. Stronger. I swam into the waters weakened, but have washed up as a monster. Bristol and Sean the Bastard here I come. These four can wait.

18

When I reach the car and sit in the driver's seat, it feels cold after being wrapped around the fire, albeit in the comforts of deception in the Governor and his crew. Their cliché gangster four-by-four Range Rover is parked on the grass verge on the opposite side of the road to the Saab. I shake my head at it and the stereotyped tragic comedy of the past few days as they've unfolded. I drive past and clip their wing mirror with as much speed as I can gather in the distance I have, which isn't much. Enough to send it back on itself as gesture to them when they return.

There's only one road in and out of the beach, the one which I've driven down; one road with a farm and a pub. Before I pass the farm and reach the pub, I decide to hide the car in the campsite alongside and wait for them to drive past and try to tail them. If I can follow them and know where they're from, I'll have it all. If not, I'll wait for opening time at the pub—after all, there are three days, and I can beckon them any time I want with this brick of a telephone.

I pull up by a gate, halfway up the road. I get out, creak open the gate then drive through, hiding the bad red paintjob of a Saab behind the thick hedgerow. I can see just about enough through the mass of entwined hedge. I lower the passenger window to listen too, in case they drive past and I miss it.

Nothing does pass, and I wait now with eyes shut, seat back, for a couple of hours, as I mull it all over again. The stink of the case and whatever the mud field I was parked in was sprayed with last clam up my nostrils; it smells of pure shit, both.

The dashboard says 7:30, and I wonder what the others have been doing all this time on the beach; scheming, gloating—a bit of both maybe. I start the car, it spins in the mud and my heart drops. Of course the rain I'd swum through and the muddy field weren't as sympathetic to my blackmail deadline, or to the aging car—I was stuck.

I open the car door, my feet sink in the wet mud and then an unmistakeable shadow of a four-by-four roars past on the other side of the hedge as I stand there, ankle deep in cold mud.

'Fuck!'

I punch the window then walk to the road to see them disappear up the road and around the corner, with a spray of mud and dirt flying behind.

'What time do the pubs open around here?!' I ask the empty field and a cow moos an answer from the next field across. Then the entire herd joins in. A beef chorus to my demise.

'What we got here then—dogging were we?' A farmer's voice says from a tractor, head poking from his cab above the hedge line. It must be feeding time, exciting the cattle.

'Stuck,' I say, whilst I consider altering my accent to make it a bit Welsh, to match his. An attempt to get some support.

'He-he. Won't be the first to get stuck in one of these fields. Up to their balls usually they are, as the others stare in though a steamed-up window.'

'Just me this time. I was having a break.'

'Break from choking chickens more like. One-man doggin'—not much point in that!' The farmer goes on and I sense I've given him his entertainment for the week. 'You might wanna pick a different colour to wear though!'

'What?' I say, feeling that this one-way banter could go on all morning, or day, if I didn't relent and join in one way or another.

'Wearing black and going back covered in your own jizzum—what's the wife gonna say when you walk back through covered in white patches like an idiot—a wanking idiot,' he says, really pleased with this one, and he bounces up and down on his seat, guffawing away like only a farmer that gets up each morning at the crack of dawn to spend his time freezing his limbs off can. Other than when they're stuck up to their shoulders in an animal, that is.

'Can you pull me off?' A Freudian slip leaves my mouth and I try to correct myself: 'Out, out—can you get me out!' My words bounce off his cab and into the field and hedges. Anywhere than resonating anything of the meaning I actually needed with him. It's for the cows.

'I'll be back here in a couple of hours to plough, so move it—wanker!' He chuckles, shakes his head and drives off.

'Good morning, fuck me,' I say to myself and the cattle, and put my head on the side of the car. I open one eye feeling defeated but see three used condoms lying on some old scaffold planks at the base of the hedge. Maybe they do dog here. I take the planks, shake loose the rubbers, whilst being careful not to touch them, and I place the planks under the back wheels of the car then slowly reverse onto and over them and out through the gate I'd left open. I drive with frustration up the lane and contemplate parking up at the campsite and pull up to the gates as the friendly-looking farmer's wife saunters over to talk about my pitch, and I realise they've taken some of the cash and left me with the white powder. I pat my coat down and find the change from a fifty that I must have put in there from a pub or the petrol station.

'Tent?' the lady smiles sweetly, making me want to move in. I instantly feel looked after.

'No tent, just car.'

'Oh, we're not a car park, you know? There are a few spaces down by the beach if you're just going for walk.' In the short exchange I question the point of it all, camping generally but more specifically me camping there when I should be in Bristol finding the girl. I had three days, which was plenty to get it all done, as long as I didn't get distracted by a drink. I decide to drive a bit up the road and park outside the pub, the Plough and Harrow.

I wait for it to open—which wouldn't be for another four or five hours. I have an old Casio wristwatch, the timepiece of terrorists and soldiers alike, and set the three-day countdown to go. It would pass me by, but it gave me something to do whilst waiting for a pint of Welsh cider. A seagull climbs up the windscreen and slides back down, twice, three times—pads its way up and slides down and I stare out at it, with both of us idling away our morning when we've bigger things to do. The fourth time it slides past my eyes I giggle to myself. The fifth time I try to flick it off with the windscreen wipers and they miss but it flies off anyway. An hour later it does a fly-by, depositing a shit like a giant swan or pterodactyl from a great height. It's quite a load and achievement and covers the entire front of the car.

An hour or so later again, and another farmer stumbles out of the pub, then back in again, that opening time was never going to come, because the pub had never been shut in the first place. I could hear cheers and see the smoke of a lock-in pushing him out into the midday sun like a ball from a cannon, stumbling out then back in again. I grab my notebook, thankful of the head start, open the car door and step towards an unspoilt Welsh drinking hole, complete with wood beams, picnic tables outside, quoits and a general, unchanged history that would surely last forever.

I intend to enter subtly, sit and drink quietly, unnoticed, and then leave, to leave it all unchanged and unmarked by my visit other than its barrels being a few pints drier. I wanted to leave it as I found it; think, drink a while, then take my scheming back with me over the bridge to Bristol.

If there was music playing it would have stopped as the door creaked open and half a dozen flat caps stopped their chatter, arms hanging in mid-air surrounded by the smoke of a hard morning and night hiding from their responsibilities. Their wives, livestock and land, all lost in a pint glass.

I stuff my notebook in my pocket, feeling too much like a reporter or policeman, neither of which would be welcome, I'm sure. I walk up to the small bar at the back and lean on it between two old men, frozen by the moment. I look at the taps and see an array of cider, ranging in strength from strong to unspecified, dry to very dry, with names to suit all manner of effects it may have or what they've been made from, other than the obvious: apples.

'Pint of Black Rat,' I ask and the non-existent music starts up again, the chatter, the movement and the mixture of Welsh twangs unsympathetic to an ignorant English ear. The two types either side of me talk over and around me, and there's a general sense of relief in the air like they were all worried an angry wife or copper might have stuck their head round the corner when I did instead. But no, it was just me, another drop out, of responsibility that is; I'm just like them, an early drinker—a breakfast thinker, needing a nip.

'Black Rat, here you go—toilet's out back,' the barman states, and I wonder immediately why anyone might say that when handing over a drink, unless it's generally understood to be savage on the arse or bladder. And it would be better to tell a person straight away rather than them get caught out, as they scramble round the stools, tables and chairs trying to find a poorly signed bit of relief, before soiling themselves—yes, I'm glad he's said it.

The sniggers from either side of me confirm it, my suspicions that the drink's a known risk—but I can't help but take the challenge. I imagine the murmurs around me are taunts from the Welsh farmers and they fill my head, all of them being against this stupid English fool who 'came over here with his balls all out, thinking he was special, dressed in black and carrying his notebook—couldn't handle his cider though could he—not the BLACK RAT!'

I take my pint and sit by the unlit fireplace, complete with horse brasses, and take out my white notebook, write, think and prepare my attack on life and this pint of Black Rat in my glass, which is first in line and is downed.

'Another Black Rat,' I say to the barman after ten minutes, with little thinking, writing or mind to my real cause completed other than this liquid challenge I'd gestated for myself. I'm surrounded by critics willing me to have shat myself already, just to make their week and have a story to tell when they get home, a story and distraction outside of their own guilt. My writing and ideas move onto how they'd found me at the beach, the rabble: the Bear, Trench Coat, the girl and the hard old Governor. It didn't take much thinking—the drugs were tracked, of course they were. The giant brick phone probably was too. They hadn't tracked me yet, only a few hundred yards up the road, as they wouldn't have expected me to drive a few feet, get stuck in a field and just go to the pub. Who would, but my mother? Well, me and a dozen barmen and barmaids of Bristol, maybe

Manchester too. When they eventually get round to looking at the tracker they'll be on the other side of the bridge and be really pissed at having to pay to get back across again and what they'll see is little progress on my behalf. So I'd guess there's a tracker in the phone for me, and one in the white block of powder for Sean the Bastard. This is all too easy.

The skies open up to welcome in the late Welsh morning outside; black clouds and a torrential downpour barricade us in, easing our guilt—might as well stay, all of us, and hit the Black Rats.

'Another one,' I repeat to the barman and out of the corner of my eye I can see money changing hands. The barman puts down some complementary nuts and crisps with this one I've ordered, and says something about loading a shotgun.

An hour later I'm bent double in the outside toilet, writing in my notebook: My arse is a shotgun and the rats have well and truly left the ship!

'Another Black Rat,' I say to the barman on my return inside, and laughter erupts all around the pub with words of 'fair play' and 'good go'.

'That cider barrel was still full when you walked in for a reason, son,' he says. 'Apple colonic was it?' And the door behinds me creaks open and I can feel a familiar shadow, overbearing and bear-like, enter the room.

'What the fuck?' the Bear says, and since I've forgotten his high-pitched voice I immediately chuckle. If I'd remembered his voice I would have also remembered his defensive reaction at it being mocked too, as he charges across the bar, wooden chairs toppling, tables shifting and the tiny pub seeming to stretch to accommodate his massive square frame.

The flat caps all around show no fear, but look on like he's one of them carrying out their will. Like a whirlwind, I'm picked up, thrust out the door into the rain where Trench Coat and the girl are standing in the rain as dark demonic silhouettes in front of the black Range Rover. The hard, old Governor is in its driving seat, in more ways than one I expect, and turns on the headlights which cut through the rain and dark cloud of the roadside to blind me.

'You lot aren't short on the theatrics—ever thought of waiting inside?' I say coldly, feeling cider-confident and in control. The Bear throws me in the back seat and joins me on my left-hand side; the other two look at the Governor through the windscreen and point at the pub; he nods back at them and they go in to keep dry.

It feels like an eternity before he turns round. Like a disappointed parent. Even then it's in slow motion—the chair creaks and the windows steam up instantly. The Bear grabs the index and middle finger on my left hand and lifts them enough to create a tension but no pain—yet. I can see the Governor means to give me a harsh warning, some pain from the Bear and a lecture, so then he starts:

'If you're no use to us, then you're no use to anyone. Right-handed are you? And he looks at the Bear...

The air freezes in the car, my eyes blacken over, the gypsy and the Viking in me stand up and step forward, one full, huge step. The Range Rover's atmosphere is changed, and an invisible storm front looms from the centre of my very being. My face washes over, carrying a fury, a violence and a force I haven't let loose fully ever, and have only used in small amounts rarely. Only when absolutely needed.

There was a presence to be feared in the car and it wasn't the Bear or the Governor's words of warning—and they knew it now, smelled it in the charged air, with the sense a fuse had been lit with the doors shut and nowhere to run.

My eyes cut through the old man's stare then move to the Bear's hand on my fingers. I notice his hand quiver a little with uncertainty, and I move my eyes slowly up to his in a warning not to do anything, then I move them back to the old man.

'For now… we're on the same side… Don't… push it,' I say, slowly, surely, and with ice on every syllable. I reach into my pocket, take out the notebook and hand it to the old man who opens it whilst trying to look composed.

'See—I've been busy, working at it. Don't get confused and push us all over board!' I remove the Bear's hand from mine, take back the notebook, slowly open the car door and walk back to the shitty red Saab. My heart is steady, in control. I'm on track and un-rattled. Before I drive away, the pub door opens and the girl and Trench Coat stand there in its shadow. They look out with eyes giving away a look of, What's transpired? It's an unforeseen situation for them.

They see the odd, troubled look I've left on the Old Man's face as he stares back out at them through the windscreen of the Range Rover. When they see him weakened, their master, their looks turn to further disbelief. This look on his face is of fear, hope and uncertainty, which has been brought on by stubborn pride caught off guard. They've charged me up and set me off into the mire—they must have some reservations and regret.

They thought I was a bird with a broken wing, but a sleeping dragon has woken up. They've seen it now. It has woken up and is driving away, leaving them to the unknown, the rain and the shit.

It seems like midnight as I'm driving south through a hurricane towards Bristol. The wind and rain batter and drill at the car windscreen in waves of rat-a-tat-tat that, whilst sounding like an army of millipedes in heels dancing on the glass, also feels increasingly like the machine guns of a yesterday I had buried out at sea. Those days in Ireland when I refused to fire back and kept my ground. Layer upon layer of rain attacks the glass as I stare out, the wipers shuddering, struggling more and more with each squeaky pass.

Before I reach the motorway, I've revisited, re-imagined, and considered the case to date, and put all the key players in their little boxes and imagined their motives and likely outcomes, with or without my continued involvement. My loyalty and commitment to a girl I don't know, Cherry, keeps my resolve and determination to seeing it all through, though.

The country roads wind on and on, as the weather continues its attempt to tear through the windscreen at me. I stare on and notice a building anxiety, a niggle, a loose thread not addressed at the back of my head. I go over it again: the case, the players, the sheer noir-dance of it all, and look for the reason behind my intuition dealing me the unsettling feeling that I haven't considered something.

Sean has been dealing drugs—check. Sean has ended up using his girlfriend, Cherry, as a drugs mule with Trench Coat, the Bear, an old, hard granddad, and another femme fatale here in 'Walesland'—check. And all this after Sean's possibly groomed Cherry from his first meeting with her. Bastard—double check. Armed Dreds in the Star & Garter, back in Bristol, see his name as mud and a reason to get frosty at the mention of it, having possibly been let down on a transaction and a deal or two by Sean—check. Bottom line: Cherry is missing, Trench Coat has been having an affair with her and was expecting her on the last run across the bridge when I turned up instead, nearly getting neutered in the process. And if she had turned up, Cherry may have just eloped with Trench Coat, leaving Sean empty-handed. But… Sean knew of an affair going on. I had heard the argument, seen the fear in her eyes afterwards, and now she was missing.

My stare widens as it hits me, like a baby sledge hammer; the darker, more obvious side to this tale I hadn't explored yet, that both Sean, certainly, and maybe the others, had let me take the car. Who knows where the Bear and Trench Coat had been as the girl was strumming herself in the room, rather than keeping guard as I was passed out on the bed. And what did Sean send me off to Wales with hidden in the car other than what he handed to me? A further setup to clean his hands, or had Trench Coat and Co. faked the concern over Cherry's whereabouts?

Had Trench Coat tried to get Cherry to leave Sean on the last run, and not liked what she'd said? Two parties at least could have put Cherry closer and easier to find than I'd thought, under my nose, bent double in the boot of the car, this car, the one I was driving—if only I'd thought of it before.

'What a fucking idiot!' I shout at the rain and slam the steering wheel, as the realisation fully hits me and I feel like a patsy, a mug, a fool. Of course I hadn't just carried of a load of fake notes like an idiot to complete a deal for Sean. What's in the boot? What's in the boot and the glove box?

'What….?!' My stare tightens and by the time I reach the motorway and I've crossed the bridge my mind has finally caught up fully with the dark hollow stare of my eyes; vessels of pure anger, deceit and sheer panic at a loss of the rose I never touched.

I'm well and truly past the bridge and have looked at the glove box several times, seen the smeared fingerprints—yes, I've seen the smeared prints, two of them running down the front of it from the handle. The possible smears of a blood-stained hand opening it and putting a murder weapon inside. I look again and again as the panic rises and the lump in my throat strangles my breath. I look once over my shoulder at where the boot is, and imagine Cherry's body bent, twisted, battered and contorted, wrapped in a carpet or blanket. The sense of hopelessness, that I may have lost any hope of finding her alive before I'd even started, simmers away in me. The anger at them all and myself for getting played steams away into an uncontrollable rage. My eyes tighten further until my blood reaches boiling point and I screech over into a truck rest-stop, skidding to a halt.

Ironically I stop for a second or two, now frozen by all this realisation, as my blood continues to boil away and I struggle to breathe… I slam at the steering wheel and jump out into the rain, rush round to the boot of the car as passing cars and trucks race past, looking on at me through the dark rain. I don't care— I need to know.

With my hands on the boot I realise this could be it for my new and old identity, a monumental mistake taking us all down. Past, present, future—all gone. No amount of explanations of best intent, if believed, would stick with the police. I had some of the money, all the drugs and maybe a body with a murder weapon in the back—what a carve-up they'd done on me, whichever party it was, Sean or the Governor's. My hand goes for the boot, and I realise I need the key from the ignition to open it.

I race back to the driver's seat, kicking the side of the car as I go, which raises the attention of a few rubberneckers from cars on the way past. If only they knew and had time to stop and see the main event as I open up my shame to the world. They'd look on alright.

I put the key in the lock and pop it open, holding the boot lid with my hand so the wind and rain doesn't blow it open, so I can do the slow reveal to myself, savouring my last moments of ignorance, moments without knowing for sure if I've the body of a beautiful girl in the boot that I could have saved...

'Sorry, Cherry,' and the barely audible words, drowned by the passing traffic, leave my lips as a raindrop hangs on my bottom lip as a glanced kiss from a chance I missed, a touch from the wind and the imagined spirit of a possible dead girl in the boot.

I open it, pulling my arm with it and I'm helpless but to look, knowing that to look won't help at all, and thinking that I should drive the whole payload off the gorge and flee into another invention of myself, one which I'm better suited to; one that stops the bad guys and saves the girl in the end.

I look on in relief but my anger doesn't subside. The boot is empty. There's still a chance for Cherry, out there somewhere. There's still a chance for her, yes, but not for them. I shut the boot and pace back, sitting down into a seat which is now wet through. I glance at the glove box and rip it open without the prior ceremony of the boot. It reveals the remnants of a fast-food burger, the greasy prints on the glove box merely sauce— a big fingers-up to my paranoia.

Although there isn't a body in the boot and a blood-stained bowie knife in the front of the car, I know there could have been. I make notes in the white notebook; a reminder or two to stay on top of proceedings.

I needed to sharpen my mind and my teeth, leading my body to follow.

Bristol is calling as I drive on. Its sirens call me like a seaman sailing onto rocks. Fully aware and resolute, I take it all in. I rebuild myself with every nearing mile, and with each inch of the city's weed-tinged, acrid air as it fills me and makes me less a seaman sailing a ship onto the rocks but more of an ice-breaker, cutting and splintering my way through. The city pulls me closer to the case, to Sean the Bastard and the girl, Cherry.

19

Sucking the same lines as anyone and everyone. Next up it's… The radio in the background hisses, introducing the next song, half in and half out of clarity. *And they're gonna get themselves arrested…* It goes on.

'They're all trying to get themselves arrested,' I mouth to the empty car, as the rain, Saab and me push on into Bristol, pull off the M4, down the M49 and onto the Portway, going beneath Brunel's lasting legacy of the suspension bridge, as it arches overhead and births me back into the city which draws me home to my cause.

Passing under the underbelly of Victorian engineering, I turn left up the monster of a steep hill and the car grunts and struggles as I change gear, pushing mine and its grinding heart on and up towards the top and the brow. The sun shines on the righteous, pretentious, and rich at the crest of the hill as I enter Clifton Village and the skies part, opening to reveal an afternoon sun and the finishing touch to a sky Constable would be okay with on an off day.

I haven't decided whether to stash what's left of the notes, brick of drugs and photo at the observatory, which is on the Clifton side of the suspension bridge, or in the Giant's Cave which has its entrance from the observatory at the top. With or without the stash planted there, the romantic side of me thinks it would make a great end scene: a gun fight at the O.K. Corral or a Holmes and Moriarty duel with me and my foe teetering on the edge of the Avon Gorge, hanging from the suspension bridge or from the Giant's Cave metal grid, under its viewing platform.

I know the drugs are tagged since the gang in Wales tracked me back to the pub, just as I was enjoying my cider colonic. It's tagged and I'm not cutting up a brick to go fingering around in their messy business—besides I might as well use it to lead them where I want. I decide to keep everything for now, use the tagged drugs to bring it and them all together at some point, controlling the other rabble as and when I need to.

Surely a careful placement, followed by a call to the police, would be all it would need. I want to find the girl in one piece first though—if she is still alive. Of course these are all just uncertain thoughts and ideas rattling round my head for now; if I have a look, taste the air, feel the ground, and examine the terrain, I know it's really my last chance to turn back; I'm at a crossroads with one foot in the devil's footprint, the other hanging in mid-air, blowing in the wind.

Besides all this though, I'm not originally from here; I'm a tourist with plenty of time—three days they said, before they call in the Manchester heavies from my past. They're idiots if they think they can control that lot anyway, and not lose a kneecap or worse. For now, I'll take in some air, see some sights, and breathe in the city from the gorge.

I park up carelessly on a triangle of grass by the bridge, bald tyres scarring the wet verge. On the road as I open the car door there's a sodden playing card face down. I turn it over expecting the joker but it's the queen of hearts. I see a sign where there maybe isn't one, keep the card and put it in my white notebook as a page mark. Part of me imagines the discarded card started life as the joker and would finish, at the end of the notebook, when I'm though, turning out to actually be an ace—all selective imagined signs and pointers, seeing meaning in an inanimate thing. Ironically a discarded card with no place in the game I was in, other than the meaning and semantics I'd just imagined and assigned to it.

'You! You can't park here!' An old sergeant major type shouts, waving a stick as he bounds across the road at me—as much as an eighty-year-old with a limp can—from the front door of his palatial old Victorian house; or maybe a hotel, it's hard to tell around here.

'I just did,' I say matter-of-factly, not meaning to sound like a smartarse and looking at the front of the car blankly, then walking off in the direction of the grassy mound and tower of the observatory above us.

'Bloody idiot. The nerve!' He attacks my back with pointed words as I walk away: 'I served this county all my life for you. You'd be speaking German if it wasn't for me!' He hit a nerve with this last piece, a vital chord, and I felt it all from a fellow serviceman, another one. Again. I turn and politely salute and give a mini bow. He could tell from my face and stance it was for real and a show of respect. He nodded and for a moment an invisible thread had joined us, a drop of blood in the soil and sands we'd marched and those between us now. If I ever saw him again, I'd buy him a sherry and hear his tale. I bet he had one or two.

He shouldn't have to put up with the stupid likes of me parking over the view, bought for him by his army pension and all his lost friends overseas, and those aging and dead already. I felt his pride. Earned—he could keep it. I needed to stand up straight, re-earn my stripes, honour and self-respect all over again in this role. I'm working on it, though, and with a Viking strength if the drunk in me doesn't sabotage it all first.

I could justify a drink at any time, like any drunk, and right now, the Corry Tap beckoned me with its cider, ales and windows you couldn't see your guilt by the light of day through. It would swallow time if I gave it a chance—I knew it. And it was just around the corner and my drunken soul could smell it. First the observatory and Giant's Cave though—I needed the fresh air before another cider-slackened arsehole, that was for sure.

I walk up the grass mound, past the polished rock slide where hundreds of years' worth of kids' backslides have slid, polishing their way down, and I walk up through the trees to the entrance to the tower housing the Victorian Camera Obscura and the entrance to the cave which winds down through the rock face of the gorge, nearly thirty metres from the top and seventy-six metres from the river floor at the bottom. I over-pay the entrance fee using folding money, which was all I had rumpled up in my coat pocket. I don't think it was a fake fifty, more likely a real fiver, but I don't stop to check and just wave my hand at the change when the dinner-lady-looking woman offers it to me. Neither of us seems bothered; she's worked there too long, although the thought had crossed my mind maybe she wasn't real, a dummy or a period-dressed mannequin.

The Camera Obscura held my attention for a minute or two with its giant, old, shiny disc. A plaque suggested art schools had used it to draw the gorge and Leigh Woods on the other side, and I tried to imagine them, pretending to nobly draw the surrounding sweeping scene when really they were just remotely peering in on Victorian courting couples. All complete with petticoats over heads, rolling round in the high grass and quivering legs, from behind the trees of the grounds opposite.

Brunel's bridge builders hadn't been of a generation to be

driving white vans with copies of The Sport or The Sun in them, page threes left open on the dashboards or discarded, half-wanked over in the woods and grounds of the mansions. So the Victorian peeping Toms would have to rely on this shiny disc, huddled together, stifling an erection or two with hands in pockets, before they left, the door opened and daylight cast shame on their stains.

I stayed long enough to savour the imagined seediness of it all and then left the darkness of the Camera Obscura room, passing through a doorway and down steps into the tiny damp rock corridor of the Giant's Cave. I realise on the stone steps again that my small tourist stop-off here is my last chance for reflection, and an opportunity just to head straight to the police.

I could simply take another boring office job, whichever they gave me to hide away in, and just shrink back into a persona that wasn't my own. I could retreat, do the proverbial right thing and just give up.

The dank corridor walls and steps weep water at me; tears for every lost soul that had ever given up before me, right here, or more drastically, taken the leap from the gorge or bridge highlighting another road on the crossroads I wasn't prepared to face. Suicide.

Rumour had it that the fall didn't kill most of the jumpers from the suspension bridge but actually they suffocated in the mud flats at the bottom. Samaritans helpline numbers adorned either side of the walkways to the bridge and down here on the lookout platform at the end of the Giant's Cave steps. By the time people get this far, I expect they're beyond considering calling a stranger for a chat, or to reconsider. I wonder if a phone number for a good local restaurant, a last meal or knocking shop would do more good. A cigarette and vending machine wouldn't go amiss either. Having decided to do yourself in, maybe a last smoke or packet of Monster Munch would do the trick. Who knows? The empty calories and new addiction might be enough to tip them enough, chemically, to rethink. Tip them the right way. Standing at the lookout platform on a metal grid hanging over the gorge, I delve into a pocket, roll and light a Golden Virginia; I needed a smoke, a drink and a think. The drink could wait.

I remember one of my only acquaintances, almost a friend, who lived in Clifton Village near where I'd parked the car. After this, I'd see if he was home from work and needed a drink. His name was Brian, a stocky character with little interest in what I did and I felt similarly about him, which suited us just perfectly. We'd ended up spending a night or two together on the tiles, as he had base level drives and motivations to his life, most notably finding where his next drink, drug or girl was coming from. Whichever was most absent from his life at the time of talking would dominate the drunken dialogue between us, and be a reason for him to berate me as if I held the key to his release somehow. A pure, self-fuelled machine, out for his own pleasure—he was never without drugs for long, and could smell a dealer in a packed, noisy club like a trained hound. He could sniff them out, communicate and score sometimes with as little as a point, wave of money and inaudible shout. I suspected we had similar pasts.

The working class and dark, dirty, clubbing sides of us anyway. I expect the only experience he would have had with the forces would have been avoiding them or the occasional scuffle with a security guard. He sensed that side of me, I knew it. We both fed off it occasionally and subconsciously, with alluded-to supposition of unsaid pasts and supposed futures.

Ultimately a night out with him came down to us drinking too much and hunting down whichever bit of the drunk, girl and drug equation was lacking in his life and needed replenishing—often it was all three, and we just got drunk. Whichever was missing always seemed the most important thing in the world at the time. Sex, money, drugs. Family and friends only seem important when you don't have them, or in my case can't acknowledge them for fear of their safety.

Sometimes, like now, on the dripping ledge, overlooking the Avon Gorge and the suspension bridge, I kid myself I didn't like my absent friends and family much anyway and like now, I'd light up, fill up, drink up and move on. How many people had stood on the bridge or right here on this spot, having lost everyone and everything and just decided to erase themselves from the possibility of ever getting them back? I owed it to them all to get this done.

I slapped the railings, self-assured I was on the right track to continue with this invented persona and take ownership of it for good. I won't just leave the situation to the police to mess up; I have the tools to do it and an inside line. Who's to say they aren't already woven into it all? My priority is to get her out alive, if she still draws breath. If not… Sean, I'm coming for you and the rest can fall like dominos around you.

I'll punch and kick at the ground of the criminals in this city and as the ground shakes, they'll know I'm here to stay. I won't get rolled by any Dreds again outside a pub in Montpelier or St Pauls. If they have any sense, and hear me coming, they'll step down, move aside, and retreat back into the underbelly of Bristol's heaving 90s drugs monster and wait for me to pass by.

20

My mind is made up as I leave the observation tower and wander back down the hill to the car. I try to remember where Brian lives. I've been to his flat several times but have never arrived or certainly left it not drunk, stoned or a mixture of both. I have a faint chemical memory coming back to me as I walk on past the car, and am sure that he is close by. And then, as I stand on the corner it comes back to me; his bedsit is one of those on the corner with a tiny Juliet balcony.

Just as I'm remembering exactly which one of these period flats is his, something whizzes past my nose and bounces across the road. It's a chunky skater's type trainer, way bulkier and padded than is needed, but they like padded-out, oversized clothes and shoes. I don't know why ill-fitting clothes should aid riding a plank of wood on wheels; all image, I guess, or maybe it helps slow you down like a parachute on steep hill descents. I look and see Brian half-dressed, leaning on his balcony two floors up. He's got a T-shirt on, stained white Y-fronts with half a bald nut hanging out the side and a look somehow of impatience and faked anger all at once, like he was expecting me and I'm late.

'Where you been, fucker? What's missing?' he says with his left hand pointing at his right which is holding an invisible pint glass. 'It's your round—you owe me a pint!' And as usual his words cut through any pretentions or faked politeness. I love and hate him all at once—a true brother of the pot and pint.

'You'll be wanting this back…' I state, picking up his trainer that had narrowly missed my head. If it had made contact it would have been a double insult as the impact would have only been half the deal—his feet stink like sweaty cheese that's been buried in shit for a decade. I pick it up by the heel as if I'm handling a dead fish.

'Just throw it,' he barks, as if talking to a child. 'Now!'

And I throw it at his balcony, missing by a complete floor and it goes in through the windows of the floor below.

'Oops,' I say, hand to mouth, faking an expression as if it were intentional. It wasn't, I just hadn't thrown anything for as long as I could remember. A look of panic goes across his face and he disappears inside his flat, the French doors clatter shut in a slam behind him and despite them being shut I can still hear a loud bang from the street two storeys down—I assume this is him falling over putting his trousers on.

I stand fixed to the spot on the road as a couple of cars drive around me and then, ten minutes later ,he emerges, like a bear from his cave, and not totally dissimilar to the one in Wales that had smacked me around the past few days—similar in stature, a stocky mass of blunt personality and shape; without the squeaky voice though, otherwise we couldn't have spent time together without me cracking up all the time.

He walks almost bow-legged, like a cowboy, swinging his legs in baggy combat trousers with skater shoes on the end. He swings them like he has oversized, sweaty balls that chafe his legs and need emptying and no doubt he would make a point of it and them several times this evening. He uses this crude reference as part of his brash demeanour and as part of his arsenal that shakes down boundaries, making and breaking friends like a bull in a china shop.

'You. Pub. Now. Pint,' he says like a caveman, immediately quenching a thirst with his words and cancelling out any resounding guilt I might have of the too many drinks I know I've had, and of those that will inevitably follow. I take a last look in the direction of the car, consider moving it or driving us towards the city centre, but it's too late, he's walking. And I'm following. We walk towards the Corry Tap and the home of the strongest cider known to humanity. Exhibition.

The darkness of the Corry Tap is comforting with its wooden walls, low ceilings and no clear line of sight to a clock or to outside. Time stops for you in there, a true escape from the trivialities of outside, leaving just you against the barrels and idle banter.

'Two pints of Exhibition—he's paying,' he states to the barmaid.

'We only do it in halves, I'm afraid. You know, it is quite strong,' she says, seriously. A word of warning she feels obligated to say to each customer, like it doesn't increase the excitement or desire to drink the apple-tinged acid anyway.

'In that case we'll have four halves, and two empty pint glasses,' Brian says, with a wink at me.

'Okay,' she says, without protest and ,as she puts them on the bar, he pours the halves directly into the pint glasses in front of her and hands the now empty half glasses back to her.

'He's paying,' he reiterates, walking off to the corner of the pub to sit and drink in the shadows. I pay, then follow him over.

Exhibition cider has no slow release. One second you're sober, the next the room moves and you are in a land of marshmallow and slopping floors like a teenager tasting their first drop. It is south-western magic and a complete curse all, wrapped up as one and never to be tipped onto an empty stomach—unless you want trouble. I hadn't eaten since a packet of crisps that I'd subsequently shat out like a shotgun after my last dose of apples. And like a true fool, here I am again, lapping at the beast's teats, laying my head in the lion's mouth as I hit it on the arse with a big stick.

Something from the hit parade sings out of the speakers as we spark up and add to the already heavy smoke that hangs in the room all around us. We're caressed by a nicotine stench both fresh and from hundreds of years of exhaling and burnt ends soaked into every corner of this little boozer. The next few hours are faded and blackened by Brian's choice to start with such a strong and large cider.

The exhibition blinkers leave our eyes by the time we've walked around the corner to The Greyhound pub—an old haunt of the local thespians, BBC execs, and a few wannabes trying to catch some attention, or looking on with jealousy at the faces from TV who are stood around talking shit, smoking, drinking and sticking to the filth-ridden, sticky carpet in there just like everyone else.

I've a vague memory of smoking a spliff on our walk around the corner and by the time I come to hunch at the bar, I don't protest Brian's claim it's still my round. Truth be told I can't remember if, or how many he may have bought since I last heard him utter this. After asking for our usual, I look down at a Foster's ashtray on the bar.

'That's weird…' I say, both to Brian and the back of the barman who's pouring our Scotches to accompany two ciders— ice in the ciders.

'What?' both of them say in unison, although Brian is a bit slow—he must be feeling the cider-spliff compilation on his lips and mind too.

'That water in the bottom of the ashtray…'

'What? What?' Just Brian says this time, as the barman puts the drinks on the bar and looks into the ashtray.

'That water or drips from beer gathered in there,' and I point at it in disbelief.

'What for fuck's sake, what?'

'It's pooled together into a shape that looks exactly like a map of Australia.'

'What the fuck, that's bizarre. What weird sign is that? We should move there!' Brian says, joining in with my surprise.

Then it hits me, around the time I notice the barman shaking his head at us, and I pick up the ashtray in my hand and tip it. The water formation doesn't move; it's a moulding, a decoration—it's a fucking Foster's ashtray. Brian starts laughing and swearing so fast I think he might soil himself. His belly laughing eventually comes to a climactic, spluttering end as he settles down, pauses and he exclaims, 'You t-w-a-t,' and draws out each letter, cutting through the air between us, and then he hangs his mouth just long enough on the last t for it to feel like he's hitting me in the face with a claw hammer.

He is the master of the single-word put-down. I quietly replace the ashtray and shake my head then turn it into a nod of agreement, and let a small laugh escape at myself too; the drunk semi-stoned twat, indeed, I confess and am sure of it. There's no hope for me or Cherry now—where am I? What am I really meant to be doing right now?

The case, my cause and my new identity couldn't be further from my mind as we head out into the black of night and head to our third pub, my local, the White Harte. Occasional glimmers of panic rise up in my mind when I momentarily think of the car, what is in it, and what might happen if it gets stolen or towed and isn't there when I get back. My conscience doesn't last though, and liquor's reason takes over and prevails each time

I try to care.

Occasionally, I look at the old Casio watch and remember I'm on a timeframe to achieve an end, and again drunk logic dictates to me that I'm as likely to pick up a clue, a smell, a trail or hear something on the street—unfortunately for my sorry liver this was probably right. If I could steer the night towards the Dreds at the Star & Garter or one of the clubs on Stokes Croft there may be a whisper of something to overhear. There would be a contingent there, involved in it all; no doubt. For now the White Harte wasn't a bad stop though and who knows, it's Sean's local too, he might be there.

We push on out of Clifton Village towards the Triangle, getting distracted by the bad student pub nearest us, not least of all because our bladders are stretched to their limits. Inside there's a huge queue for the gents and no one stood at the urinal. There's one cubical in there that's occupied by a student girl doing tricks for cash; a big queue, one cubical, tough times, and a bad pub.

We leave, despite Brian's interest in joining the wrong queue, and head for the White Harte instead. I wonder if the writer, Paul Benjamin, would be there again—I could have a few extra notes to give him; true tales in detective noir. We seem to glide along in a beered-up, drunken time pocket which speeds up one second and is delayed an eon the next, and all the time we walk into the night and I don't feel my feet even touch the ground.

Despite the drunken barrage all around us in the streets, as herds of students clamour over each other as they pile in and out of doorways to get to their distraction from studies, and to piss their student grants and parents' mortgages up the wall, the dark, damp streets seem to sound quiet—or this is at least the illusion created before we open the door to the White Harte and its roaring mass inside.

The lights, smoke, and sounds jar us awake as the door slams behind us. It's hard to tell if there's a fight in the pub or not, as the music is loud, people scream over the top of it all and the mass of people move in waves, sometimes together, sometimes as factions as they butt up against one another.

'I'll get us a pool table, must be your go—I'll be around the corner,' I say to Brian, who's already feigning disbelief at the fact he should be expected to buy a round. I turn and walk around the corner before he has time to turn his fake protest into influencing me to shed more fake notes, if I have any, or whatever now accompanies them in my pocket as the heavy change from our night so far weighs me down.

I get my white notebook out of my pocket, hold it to my face and make an overambitious scribble or two, given the surroundings and my condition. I look over to the spot where Paul Benjamin, the writer, was sitting the other day. I think I see a version of him and salute my notebook at him like we're now joined as brothers of the pen. He sees me looking through the mass, someone knocks into his table, drops are spilt and he looks back, raising his hands, head shaking and mouthing the words: 'What's the point?' As he does, I feel sorry for him and his writing, missing the reality of it all, criticising the material all around him, as he's resisting life and all whilst writing his fiction—he might as well be holed up in a study somewhere, typing away, safe in a bubble of idle writers' freedoms.

But then it strikes me; maybe his writing is real, maybe he's documenting more than I think—me even—and maybe he thinks the same of me as I get my notebook out scribbling over here and there. He's not to know I'm on a case; maybe this is some kind of writers' duel, as we write each other in and out of existence from a distance over a crowded pub?

'Wake up.' Brian clicks his fingers in front of me, pulling me out of my thoughts as they spiral out of sense. 'Take your pint.'

And he hands me a drink off the table I'm leaning against and we both look over to the near pool table. Our attentions quickly shift to a comical fight of sorts that's broken out and building up to a breaking point. Words have been exchanged over whose table it should have been and they've gone past simmering point. Pounds have been put on the table, in a virtual queue, and some of these coins have been respected—some haven't.

The students peck at each other like hens, hackling up, strutting back and forth and pecking back out with words and their chins as their heads bob. It seems to be four of them, two against two. It makes us laugh, so we get closer to the virtual front line. Brian grins in anticipation. Fact is he could snap them all like twigs so he could safely stand in the middle of the fighting ring as the tensions unfold. Me too, but he knew nothing of my past, and I was happy to keep it that way.

If I'd ever slipped anything of myself out whilst blind drunk, chances are he will have been at the same time too, and he would have let it pool together with the other made-up shit he was so sure fell from my mind and mouth—it entertained him to hear and me too to escape in the invented chat. Now I was living it though, and my case was hot. I would use Brian as an unknowing ally and a first line of defence—a bodyguard I might not need but would enjoy the company of for now.

I can't see Sean the Bastard in the furore that's forming, so I join Brian in his front row position and wait for the fighting to begin. Heads bob again, fingers prod into chests and lit cigarettes point at faces; all just piss in the wind and hot air.

We think it's all going nowhere as Brian and I look at each other in consolation of the damp squib of a situation before us. Just as we turn to leave, one of the strutting hens' girlfriends comes over and another hen pushes and shoves her out of the way—and that's it. The catalyst—the fuse is lit.

A pint is thrown, then a fist. Beer flies in the air as Brian and I laugh and slap our thighs. A cap is taken off someone's head, thrown to the floor and stamped on, and a cheek is punched but only a half-pulled punch—they couldn't hit themselves with any real vehemence, they didn't know how. Paper tigers, teenagers who'd drink too much, some with a bruised ego, in front of a pretty girlfriend, as they wait for a turn on a pool table. They rock and roll back and forth, knocking tables, people and chairs. A pool cue is picked up and swung, again not with any real intent other than show. Brian and I walk coolly around the table, insert someone's pound and rack the table up. Around us the pseudo fight escalates as furniture's pushed over and a chair is picked up to throw.

'Where's the fucking black?' Brian asks looking down at the triangle all neatly set up, less the key ball to the game. He looks up and around the room this time holding his hands out. 'Seriously, where the fuck?' He moves his head back to avoid another timidly swung cue, with his hands still outstretched gesturing for the missing ball. Pool balls join the fight, added to the arsenal, and are thrown from one side of the room to another. We duck as the missiles fly and Brian's hands remain on the table top. A ball rebounds off the ceiling, hits a light and lands square in his palm. It's the black. Time stops and smoke settles in the air at the poetry of it all.

'Did that just happen?' I say, smiling, accompanied by a chuckle of disbelief and an appreciation of the true surreal madness. Brian just looks at his palm, shaking his head. The fight stops all around us. Three or four guys near us look on at us in disbelief, as does the girl who had inadvertently kicked it all off. I suddenly become aware the music has been stopped and the staff have joined the room, all in their little black shirts, to split up the fight, which has already fizzled itself out. Their timing is that of cowards or spectators, only showing their true colours after the show has ended. I'd seen that before, all too often. Most of the room is now looking at the pool table, Brian's hands and me with mutters of, 'What the fuck just happened?'

'I think it's your table next,' Brian says, dropping the black in its rightful place and picking up the remaining cue on the table and handing it to the nearest person. Then we down our pints and leave like priests of misdirection and drunk fight referees, both of us in total disbelief. Somehow we carry it out with us like we had actually orchestrated it all—masters of the ceremony.

21

I wake up on Brandon Hill; the picturesque, high, grassy mound on the side of Park Street in the centre of the city. The grassy hill is complete with a giant old church, now converted into a concert hall, and intricate Zen-like pathways around a series of fish ponds at the top, Cabot Tower, an old folks' bowling green, views as far as Glastonbury and down to the SS Great Britain and the dockside cranes. All this picturesque tourist trap collection, and me in a heap at the top of the hill, on a patch of grass normally used by courting couples, peeping toms spying on the courting couples, or teenagers smoking weed.

My beer-soaked, blurry eyes start to make out the outline of a squirrel which is an inch or two from my face. I feel down my leg to my right foot which is damp and missing a trainer. My head pounds with guilt, pain, confused memories and something else—probably shame.

Pictures and thoughts after the White Harte, the flying eight ball and semi-fight are incomplete, broken, vague, and not pieced together—like me. As I sit up, I wheeze out the stench of my insides; the air, smoke and polluted essence of the night before which disturbs a nearby family who have been having a picnic a few yards away, until my hangover breaks their serenity like a fart in library.

The mother subsequently ushers the children away with one

child looking like they might cry, and the other holds in a laugh. I can't see the dad; maybe he's chatting up an ice-cream lady or cottaging in the top toilets. Who knows how these family outings actually work past the sightseeing, scorned looks, and mud on knees? I'm only ever a witness.

I've a vague memory of the Hatchet, a pub on Frogmore Street and maybe one or two on old King Street but then it seems we went to Belgo which is off Queen Square. I remember ordering something from Belgium with a weird name: Satan's Piss, Devils Run-off—something along those lines. And again although served in smaller bottles, Brian insisted we have them decanted into pint glasses—game over, the end, goodnight ladies and gentleman. Until I wake up now with a pig having shat in my head, missing a shoe and all the muddled memories to show for it.

I flick through the notebook, which has a page or two of shorthand drunken hieroglyphic scribbles, some of which confirm my initial thoughts, but others alluding to a bigger picture, a club after the last pub and maybe more. I'd have to recheck my notes when the fog behind my eyes has cleared.

First I need to get back to the car, if it was still there. The car, the flat and the case I was on. It's a steep walk down the hill and another up Constitution Hill to get back into Clifton Village; steep for a normal person, but nearly a marathon for my polluted bones carrying yesterday's binge.

I see my missing trainer bobbing around in the weeds and scum of the fish pond as I stumble onwards. I creak down to stretch and pick it out of the water, which makes every ounce of me ache and sends me a flash of faintness across my eyes—I nearly black out. I squelch my right foot down into the sorry insole and water oozes out which is cold and satisfying, like squeezing an overdue boil or spot.

I bound on down the hill helped largely by gravity, momentum and the grass, avoiding the occasional pile of shit left by a dog. By the time I hit the bottom path, I stop for a breath and read the ancient old sign on the stone wall that reads: NOTICE. NO CARPET BEATING ALLOWED BEFORE 6AM OR AFTER 9PM.

I look at my watch, which reads 11.30am and brush myself down, leaving twigs, soil and bits of tobacco to fall to the path at my feet.

Constitution Hill is my last challenge before getting back to Clifton and the car. Ridiculously steep for a car let alone me. I stop again, look at it, wishing myself to float effortlessly up it on an invisible conveyor belt, but it doesn't come. The Hope and Anchor pub opposite almost draws me in for a hair of the dog, as I pause to summon the strength.

Good intentions and indecisiveness win out, and I push on up the big bastard of a hill instead, pulling my body and heavy legs through air that feels as thick as treacle. As I lift each leg it's as though I'm on the moon or pulling my feet from mud. By the top I'm smiling. I realise that I'm grinning—not through any self-awareness or joy, but when I see the quizzical looks from the handful of passers-by. It can't be the first walk of shame into Clifton Village and up this hill, but it doesn't stop the condescension and look of judgement from the old, retired and pompous as they pass me by.

As I cross the brow of the hill and the incline lifts, I feel like I'm on air and I glide through the old streets, past the bakers, coffee shops and delis. A hop, skip and a hungover jump into the heart of Berkeley Square then onto where the car resides. My walk slows as the worry grows in me about the state of the car— is it still there? In one piece? Clamped? Ticketed? Towed?

I pass the scene of the start of the crime that was the night before, below Brian's flat, and I see the car in the mid-distance. It's taped around once in police blue and white ribbon and a small plastic yellow envelope is stuck to the windscreen. I feel relieved: it's there still, in one piece, with a semi-flat front tyre, but I think that was there to begin with.

I rip at the tape and flick it off my fingers to the floor then take the yellow envelope from the windscreen, open my white notebook and put it in the pocket at the back. A police notice might come in handy at some point, and I may be able to tailor it to look like an official demand to my needs at the time.

I can see the black holdall is still in the passenger footwell as I open the driver's side door and slouch in, relieved and feeling more than a glimmer of good luck. I inspect the bag; it's all there, all the drugs, brick phone, clothes and my mission. Unbelievable, I think, as well as wondering: Did part of me secretly really want it all gone from my life? To let it dissipate like a bad dream, purged by my night drowned in cider?

I start the car which splutters to life. It's reliable, despite its age, haggard appearance, and treatment—just like the rest of us. I indicate and rev the engine to drive off as a black mass of coat and legs stirs on the back seat and a Disney-Chinese-looking young girl who looks like she's used it for a bed for the night is woken up. Her blurry eyes part to reveal what I assume is another hangover to fill the car, although I stink so much of booze, another one to fuel it would go unnoticed. As she groans back to life I look at her bare legs and small black dress which is almost riding too high above her arse. I feel nothing; she must only be eighteen, nineteen at most—a child.

'Can I help you!?' she snaps, watching me, watching her. A stern look up and down at me with confidence. Maybe she's older. I start to feel something, dulled by drink but something, and I smirk. It must look seedy from outside so I stop.

'Are you staying or coming?' I ask to the mass of leg, dress and coat.

'I'd like to do both—but NOT with you!'

'Get the fuck out then,' and I thumb towards the door, turn around in the seat, rev the engine again. And, in a flash of black, like a crow taking flight, she's gone. Too swift and assured to have been drinking and sleeping rough the night before. Too sure and flying straight for that.

I felt uncertain of my presence; she wasn't all that surprised or uncertain herself, I could just tell. It's easy to recognise what's missing in yourself when it's highlighted by someone else, thrown at you out of the blue like that by someone who's all still intact. When her door is slammed shut I notice something sweet in the air momentarily overpowering my stench as it leaves with her, fragments and a wisp blown back in on the wind as the door shuts: CK One, L'Eau d'Issey or similar.

Again, I recognise it from something now absent from me and my life that used to mean something. A smell. A memory. A person absent, lost but not forgotten. I pull away from the curb, Clifton and the night's wasted time pissed away when I should have been doing something else. Looking at my watch I can see it's dead but I know I've got a day or two.

Two days left! Focus starts to return and I decide to drive back to the flat. I'll let myself into Sean's flat before mine, confront him, maybe find Cherry tied up, beaten or worse in there or just plant the stuff in his space, lay low in mine with my ear to the floor. I'm John Barrie et al., apparent PI. On the case and back on track.

I try to drive with my eyes blurring in waves, as a sweat builds on my head in layers, on top of the perspiration from climbing up Constitution Hill. Anxiety flows out of sync with my eyes and I become increasingly aware of my driving, trees, parked cars, pedestrians and I imagine accidents happening before I've got close enough to the hazards themselves. I rummage for a spare miniature from the hotel in the bag. Nothing. No respite.

I pull past the corner of my flat, the barometer shop and the graffiti of the girl and balloon. Someone has signed off Banksy and it reminds me of the office and the office job I'd escaped, just like a bank. I wonder if the person's tag is a rebellion against a formality, a celebration of it or just a play on a shortened surname. By the time I've pondered it I've nearly hit two cars, a wheelie bin and driven over some bags of rubbish down the steep cobbled hill off Lower Park Row. I'll dump the car here behind the wall at the back of the flats. Sean won't bother coming round here or see it from his window. That and I might need it to escape at the drop of a hat. Up close to the graffiti I can see some bored kid or drunk has tried to scribble a W over the B in Banksy. A losing battle of Biro versus spray can.

I pick up the bag, kick the car door shut and walk around to the front door without making any attempt to hide myself. If I'm seen, I'm seen, and the confrontation can start then and there. If not, I'll play it out, spy for a while and see what or who he's got trussed up in his flat. I'm still all in black borrowed clothes, stained with sea, sand, blood, piss and beer but still black enough to blend into a shadow, to look casual in a pub. To look like a hungover PI skulking back to his cave which is all I am at most. I need a shower. The adventure stings my eyes so far and there's more to come. First I need to see if Cherry is in her and Sean's flat, alive and ready to leave.

I ease the key into the main front door like I'm picking it. I feel the latches of metal stroking the sides of it as it slides in to a click felt, not heard, as it makes it home to the back of the lock.

I nudge it quietly round, as my arm and hand tenses. It pops, falling open half a foot and is stopped by the ever shifting and evolving pile of mail. Already, on the top, I can see a familiar envelope for me. I'd received them leading up to the case and then an anonymous note pre-empted Sean's knock on my door that started all this. It's possibly from the same person. Maybe they're all idle crazy random notes from me, written before I fully broke down at work. Maybe I put them in the outgoing mail pile, dated for future despatch.

I push the door and mail that's behind it far enough that I can slip in like a shadow cast in from the street—with no sound. I stoop, pick up the brown envelope to savour later, squeezing it into the black bag and zipping it back up.

Now, first stop: Cherry-picking. That is if there's anything left on the tree that hasn't been bruised. Has Sean got her up there in his flat? Did he send me into the Welsh uber-corporate hotel under the pretence of getting her back, when he just wanted his deal done with the trench-coat-wearing gibbon, the bear-sized, high-pitched mass of a man and the wanking femme fatale?

I peer under my belt line at their memory, bound forever and cut into my flesh as my taped-up manhood. I also look in the top of the bag at the massive brick phone—which never rings. By the time it does it'll be too late for someone: Cherry, if not already, me if the three days are up and too late for them if they've made a call to my past associates in Manchester—they'll kill us all, rip the town in two and cruise back up the M5 like they've been on a picnic in the park. They'll tear us apart, a wind blowing through the streets, leaving me as the dead pariah who tried to do well. And them all; from across the bridge and Sean the Bastard, they'll be savaged by them as stupid little boys who'd played too long pretending to be gangsters—all out of their depth. And the girls. I'm not thinking about what they'd make of the girls.

I climb the worn-out blue carpeted steps, trying to remember the squeaky ones. It's no good; I don't hit them all but in between my squelching right foot, still damp from spending the night in the fish pond at the top of Brandon Hill, and the creak of the old wooden stairs under foot, I might as well have shouted up the staircase, 'Hi, honey, I'm home!'

Three storeys up and I hover outside Sean's door. The next chapter is waiting to unfold, the next test of my determination and skills in this new self-made role. I put the bag down slowly, letting my ear brush past the door as I do, listening all the while. I stay hunched over with an ear to wood. It's a hollow fibre door, with no substance. If a mouse farts in Sean's flat, I'll be able to hear it. I can't hear a thing, but hold the position long enough for my lower back to burn in protest

Now to break in. The doors and locks here are feeble. No one had much to steal or what was worth stealing was the same as everyone else. Except Sean—he had drugs, money and a tied-up girl (maybe). Well he did have the money and now the drugs; they've been all been on holiday but they're home now. A plant—I'd hide them in his own place if I could get in. That way when the others trace it they can bust his balls, not mine again.

I push at the door and can see the door latch through the frame. I check my pockets for my wallet. Did I even have a wallet, any ID? I can't remember. In my back pocket I find a student NUS ID card and get a flashback to last night; Brian mumbling something about needing to get his hands on an NUS card to get access to all the cheap drinks, clubs, student nights and student girls. I don't want to remember any more. I shake my head trying to cast out the bad spells and ashamed potential memories, and hope it's just something I found in my sleep. The

NUS card is laminated and slim enough to edge down the frame and tease the lock open. I do, open it and step in.

The full-height bay windows, same as my flat, shine over a table covered in random shit—flyers, bottles, tabloids and mail. It's so similar to my own place, I stop for a second to make sure it isn't. A smell of food, aftershave and a life lived lets me know it's not. There's too much love and life in the air even if it's to and from Sean the Bastard himself. I doubt he even had any feeling left for Cherry at the end of a day. Not a drop.

I walk slowly, rolling on the balls of my feet; only a slight squelch left resounding from the right. Like a prowling leopard sneaking up on its prey, I move on through, feeling each breath leave my body. I'm taut and tense with each step, in anticipation of what might be around the corner, falling from a cupboard or hiding under a table.

I place the bag and brick phone by the table and move to the small, empty corridor joining the front room kitchenette and living space to the bedroom and bathroom at the back. The door at the end of it is shut and my heart speeds up; a lump in the throat swells as I go for the handle. Is she here? Is he here? Is she dead on the bed, bound up tight in the wardrobe? Can I rescue the girl and ride off into the sunset, case closed, as a knight in shining armour?

I ease the handle down, it creaks in protest and a stale air and smell escapes, strong and old enough for me to sense over my own: sex, bodies, sweat and something else. I feel a wave of panic rise in me but control it, holding it down for now. Impatience and a feeling that I don't want to be too late if I need to help unbind, untether or resuscitate pushes me on.

An image of my lips on hers transcends rescue as I push it fully open, revealing a cheap double bed up against the right-hand wall, duvet sheets and clothes half on and half off the bed.

I close the door behind me to reveal a spray of blood across the wall. It starts at her height, 5'2", and then it's sprayed with the force of a hit, a push, a punch, a smack on top of a cut all the way up the wall. The paint is peeling nearer the top and some blood has gone under the flakes of paint that are lifting, making them look like flaps of skin, like the wall itself is wounded.

I step closer, my nose an inch away. I slowly close my eyes and feel everything there is left in the room. The blood is black, maybe from the night after I heard them fighting. There's enough of it to be a hit onto a gash or wound. A hit on top of a hit. Imagining his vain fists pounding mindlessly into her makes me boil inside. An urge to wring his neck, popping his eyes, vividly builds and ripens in my mind.

I scan the room for anything else, then walk to the dark wooden wardrobe and stand there, full to the brim with apprehension and dread—I wait in front of it, like it's my own coffin, ready to open up and swallow me whole. There's another patch of blood on the handle which adds to the self-admission—I'm just too late.

I'm too late, I'm sure, and this game is going to evolve into a revenge mission at the swing of this door. I know it now. I breathe out slowly, holding it there in mid-air, long enough to feel time stop. I then breathe it all back in and with a gasp and a jolt I yank the door open.

22

There's no body. There is a patch of blood on the inside of the door, a pile of wire and plastic coat hangers in a tangled heap that would test the patience of anyone to dismantle—but there's no body. A single hanger is left holding a lonely red dress, torn a little, short and enough for me to imagine how radiant and room-stopping she must have looked in it—but nothing else.

Despite the fear she might not be alive, the image of her stops me solid in my tracks, as the power of her female form takes over my senses of place and time. It looks like someone's cleared everything out in a hurry, kept the dress as a souvenir maybe. It's gut-wrenching, framed by the open door of the wardrobe, a show stopper for now and, again, I'm frozen by the image, the poetry and the implications. This time it's physical and in front of me, not imagined. There's no easy ending I can see for me or any of the players in the game now, not here, not anywhere.

I walk back through to the kitchenette and front room and look in the half-height fridge, partially for my stomach but mainly for further investigation. There are some leftovers from some time ago. I guess cooked by her. A pile of three sorry ready meals, which must be his attempt at domesticity, which lets me know he's still potentially using this place as a base. The fact he threw out the clothes but kept the leftovers from a week ago lets me know how ancillary the fridge's function is to his life; just a holding cell for his pre-processed faeces.

I pick out a jar of hotdog sausages and eat them raw as I walk back over to the table and back, thinking, pacing and piecing it together. There's a labelled bottle of vodka and a glass on the table which I consider to be a potential trap, then justify it to myself under the premise of Sean the Bastard not being thoughtful enough to have conceived of such a thing—me breaking in.

I pour a healthy dose of what's probably an economy brand to him but a labelled expense to me, and knock it back as I now consider my next move. I stare out the window and notice the lights coming up, the flames rising again, only this time I feel everything: the pulse, the rise and tide, flowing through the floating harbour, life blood of the city—I feel these lights now, the flames building and I'm the torch bearer.

I look at my watch, which is an empty gesture as it's stopped displaying anything of sense, all alien digital blurb to me. But I am aware of time passing as I've seen the outside changes in orange hue, and I wonder does he, Sean, have a routine, a day job? When would he return? And if he did while I was there, then the confrontation would just have to start early, wouldn't it? I'd have to dig in, hit back as an internal force or hide and pick at him like a parasite from his own ground.

The bag is at my feet and is stretched tight with the brick phone, clothes and block of drugs. I crouch down on my knees and unzip it and I almost feel its relief as it eases open, spilling its guts and mine like a septic wound. Everything here could make or break me now and I know it. I rummage down into it, pushing generic black clothes to one side until my hand lands on the cellophane white brick of drugs—the orphaned produce of Brazil, or similar, now passed around in this power play in

Bristol's criminal scene. I take it out, hold it long enough in my palm to feel the evil—all those hurt for it from plantation, transportation, laboured over by beaten kids, through to my cut-up scrotum and my bruised jaw—all that done and will be done for this brick of shit and the girl, Cherry. I feel it all just for a moment; life's beauty and the beast.

I get the tape out that I'd used to bandage up my old chap, and I lie on my back with the tape and brick in each hand. I squirm backwards, like the worm I am, under the dining table in front of the windows. I hold the evil white block up to the centre of the table's underside, then use my teeth to find the end, and stretch out a bit of tape.

Fixing the block in place, I think what better a place than right under his nose to stash that thing he wanted over life itself, over his own piece of true beauty. Yes, a perfect place right here, right now, on his own table's underbelly. When he gets back and wonders where I am, wondering if I've completed the mule run or got messed up, it'll be here right under the bastard's own face.

Another length, and it's fixed good and tight. I prod it with a finger for no other reason than to sense it, frottage it—the tightly wrapped and suspended little package of pain. As I wriggle my way back out, forward this time, through roach ends, Rizla papers and loose tobacco discarded to the floor, I shake my head at the similarity to my own place. As I squirm my last half foot, a half-smoked, mini, carrot-shaped joint catches my eye—a bonus for my efforts—and I pick it up and put it behind my ear.

I slowly rise, feeling like another important piece is in place, even if the most important, Cherry, is likely gone, dead and buried. If I could get out and hang out in my flat for a bit, just long enough under the radar of Sean's attentions, I could orchestrate everything so it points back to him—then make the call when I'm ready and end this, for good, all of it—for him anyway, the murdering drug dealer. I'm sure of it.

I pour another healthy dose from his bottle, knowing I'd have to top up its level now with water if it was to go unnoticed. My stomach gurgles with the raw acid of the vodka as it mixes with the also raw sausage meat from the jar that I'd devoured from the fridge earlier. I stare out at the city again, take the joint-end from behind my ear and look over the table's mess for a lighter. There's half a book of matches on top of a flyer for the Bierkeller—a dark, sweat dripping off the walls, goths and punks kind of place. Scribbled on the flyer, which is for tonight, it says CHINA BOB, TONIGHT! and my heart drops…

I'd heard of China Bob from my days back when I was working on the doors of the Manchester clubs. I'd heard of China Bob alright. He had a reputation; cold and emotionless, disarmingly slight of frame, solid muscle no fat—a true killer, a doer, an odd-job man to call on.

Problem often was for his employers that when they did, and wound him up, they had to just let him go and run his course. He didn't have an off switch. If Sean was arranging to meet China Bob, I could only assume it was to find me, get the shit back and for it to be over my broken bones or worse. When Sean started me up on this case, I was just the drunk next door though, a patsy, a tattered dog he'd thrown a stick for and said 'fetch'. I might have gone over the bridge like that but I've returned hardened, a culmination of my past training, and as a force of nature.

I clench my fists at the glory of it all. I would get to take them all down. I look out the window as a smile creeps across my face, hands clenched. The city lights reflects across my eyes, but my stomach gurgles again, interrupting any further grandiose stance on my behalf.

I feel movement down in my guts and I know, after a further bubbling, that I have to go! I have to shit and I have to shit right now! I grab the matches, flyer and glass and run down Sean's corridor, past Cherry's spray of blood up the wall and then to the bathroom. My trousers and pants are down in a blink and the seat cracks against the enamel rim as the full weight of my body lands, feeling the force of my arsehole as it fires vodka, cider, residue of crisps and raw sausages; expelled, sprayed and delivered to my foe's toilet bowl.

Despite the lack of applause, I feel a certain sense of a show well done; I'd be good to the interval at least. I break open the match book, light up the spliff and take in almost all of what's left in its limp shaft in a single breath. A deep blanket spills over my insides. I'm done, and I stand, calmly throwing the butt into the mess left by my toilet terrorism.

Then I walk through, put the flyer and matches back on the table, pick up the bag and leave without flushing. A risky statement I'm sure, but can't recall if it was clean or flushed when I attacked, so I take the risk. I shit at him now and would bring the true storm later for Cherry. I stretch my muscles to full capacity, as they start to remember what they can be.

For now, I'd lie low downstairs in my flat, keep an ear out and head for the Bierkeller later. China Bob and Sean the Bastard would wait till tonight. An easy play; time now for a stoned rest. The drugs are planted, the phone ready to call to get the rest involved and my cock must be nearly healed. I put fresh tape over it, then lie down. I would listen, wait, then I'd launch into the night; at them, him and all of it. I'd push China Bob aside, and wring it out of Sean what he's done with her—the stupid vain bastard. My first case was dirty, hard on the body and would sting by the end.

Back in my own flat, it takes me a while to adjust. The

similarities to Sean's flat and the mess make me certain for the first few minutes that I've been rolled, broken into, burgled, and searched by someone. Slowly and surely, though, the stoned realisation creeps over me that this is just how I've been living. There's no order, no place for things. No folded things here and there slotted into their own little homes.

I lie back on the bed, open the white Moleskine and create an order to things on the page. I write up my thoughts, those been and gone, and ideas on those to come. It flows from me like a stream. The written order gives me calm in amongst the room's chaos. My eyes close, hands wrapping the elastic around the notebook and I listen out, scanning for any movement coming from above in Sean's flat.

I dream, I regenerate, and rebuild myself for the fight ahead of me. For the girl, Cherry, and my future. I see myself back on Brandon Hill, at the top of the old Cabot Tower, on top of the city's green haven and viewing station. I'm overlooking it all from the SS Great Britain down to the waterfront and the dockside cranes, the industrial sheds, and rows of terraced houses where workers once lived after spending their days toiling away in the giant red cubes of the giant red square tobacco factories around them. I see it all undulating and breathing to and fro in front of me.

In a breath, the city sucks me down the narrow staircase of the tower and stops me at the edge of the Zen-like fish ponds. Wooden walkways grow out in front of me as I walk across them. I feel I'm everywhere and nowhere in the city. I'm a wind and a ghostly minder, here to look after its vulnerable. I pass the second pond and I look down to see it's full of right-foot trainers. I look up and laugh at the lucid moment's connection to reality.

A fish jumps, spilling the shoes to one side and as it lands there's a splash of laces and soles. In a blink, the girl from the graffiti I'd seen by the flat appears with her red balloon at the end of the wooden walkway that I'm standing on. She looks worried and scared and her voice trembles.

'No future,' she mutters, lip trembling and tears pooling in her eyes. I move towards her slowly, not wanting to scare her any more than she is already. I want to look after her, make things alright for her and this city.

'No future, sir?' she says again, and this time it sounds like an offer, an option or a possibility...

'We'll see,' I say, with all my heart and sincerity to comfort her. 'We'll see... Cherry,' as I see the similarity and what she symbolises to me now.

She smiles and runs towards me, her little red balloon trailing in the air behind her and I take her gently by the hand. We walk over and off the walkways of the pond and onto the grass mound at the top of the hill. The grass, daisies and dandelions crack, crush and splinter like hard candy under our feet, like they've been frozen by dry ice.

We stand on the grassy mound looking down through the trees of Brandon Hill. She's scared again as she sees movement, her hand trembling, shaking at the shadows and silhouettes moving between the trees at the bottom. There's the unmistakeable outline of a huge man, the size of a bear. The Bear, Trench Coat, the girl from Wales and the old Governor with a stick are all there.

The little girl grips my hand tightly and I tell her not to worry. I stare down at them all and they just wait for us, watching. By the kids' playground at the bottom, there's the black silhouette of Sean the Bastard. He's smoking a cigarette, not looking at us, but looking across at the swings and kids' castle where a slight of frame and tense character, even from this distance, is standing bolt upright—it's China Bob. He stands like a statue, inviting us and warning us off all at once.

'I'm scared,' the little girl whimpers.

'Don't be,' I say looking down at her. 'Look over there,' and I point over to the right where Sean is looking now, about fifty metres away by an oak tree—it's the Viking, and it's also me: as one.

Sean looks on, hesitant, and so does China Bob; in slow motion they all slowly notice my alter-ego and the Bear, Trench Coat and the rest, all of their silhouettes turn to face the Viking. China Bob ushers my warrior on with a two-handed 'bring it on' gesture, and Sean the Bastard flicks his cigarette in the air. The red tip of the stick as it flies is the only colour against their black outlines. Before the fag hits the floor we turn.

We turn before the fight ensues and before the outcome is suggested. I take the little girl away from it and we walk back over the other side of Brandon Hill and past the tower and through the trees. We leave the warrior to it and the outcome left unknown for now. We pass a man on a bench scribbling in a notebook and I recognise him from the White Harte as Paul Benjamin. He looks up and hands us the book and his pen.

'Future won't write itself,' he says flatly and coldly to me. 'Have my pen.'

I take it, open my coat and put it in my inside pocket. I nod as we pass him by and head on into the canopy of the trees where squirrels scamper and dart between the trunks. One stops halfway up a trunk and looks at us both with black empty eyes. The girl then points and chuckles, sending the grey tree-rat on its way. We pass an ice cream truck which jingle-jangles a tune that sounds like something more for a rock festival in Brazil than a park. The jingle-jangle of its musical call dances all around us in the air, and although there are no words to its instrumental childish rendition, I know it and I remember the tune, I know the anger and ferocity in it and my dreaming mind sings the lyrics out, quiet at first, building up and up until it's a screeching shout and a yell as the tower, the mound, the trees and girl dissolve all around me. They all disappear as the lyrics build louder and louder until I wake:

Untethered... Now to be transformed, reborn, rebuilt and remade.

And in a flash and shudder, I see them coming at me; lunging, swinging, some with guns and sticks. They've got knives and blades too as they flash before me and I snap awake, to an empty room.

I sit bolt upright and utter the final lyrics: 'For some lost soul's sake!'

For some lost soul's sake.

23

With a rush and a push, the land and city will be all mine. I'll charge out the door, into the streets and I'll re-take the night. Tonight. The people with burdens of guilt in this caper will all fall, and the rest will witness my new identity and arrival. I'm charged up and ready to race at Sean with iron fists. Why did he do it to her, the blood up the walls and the hastily emptied wardrobe with only a sleazy red number of a dress left behind?

Maybe he'd kept it to wank over, indignant at her behaviour perhaps? All whilst he thought and stewed over it: how dare she cheat on him? How dare she cheat on him with another dealer? Maybe he'd omit the fact Trench Coat was just another dealer; one better-looking, stronger and less vain. No doubt he'd omit that too—all that, but he is a dealer, still the same and would be going down with him too, if I could come through this on top.

I'm up and ready despite a cold mist in the flat which is made worse, emphasised by each breath. It must be 7 or 8ish in the evening. I'll need to check the time for sure, if I am to start the night as though I'm actually in some sort of control of the situation and outcome—even if my beer-battered internal compass means, inevitably to improvise its own internal route, pushing me into the shadows where liquid and bodily demons will wait. And attack.

I root around in the bag for any remaining notes and bundle

what's left of them into my pockets then take the phone out too, inspecting its oversized case and battery level, which is half full. It's full enough for what it needs to do. Like me, it's half full but not finished. Not yet.

I pause and listen for anything from the floor boards above. Nothing. Not a mouse, needle drop, rustle or a stir. If Sean had returned and discovered someone had redecorated his toilet, I would have heard it. I remember the envelope addressed to me that was on the mat downstairs. I rise like a Kraken slowly from the bed, but strong. I grab my notebook, splash water on my face and head through to the bag in the front room.

I take out the envelope. Waiting with bated breath I finger the sealed edge. It feels like it could mean all or nothing to me. If I've been writing these notes to myself then it could appear as idle irrelevance or an insane reminder, enough to drag me back into the bowels of my insanity before it gives birth to my new purpose. Or what if it's from Cherry before her blood covered Sean's wall? I check for a dated stamp on the front and there's nothing: no print, mark or pointers. Just a hastily printed name: mine. I dispense with any further imagined anxiety and pain, and tear it open like it's a last fix, a last meal and an answer from beyond the grave—if it is actually from Cherry. I drop out another single sheet of A4 from inside to the table top, face up.

The early evening's street lights flicker across the page before the individual letters become clear and I start to read. Police sirens drive past the front of the building, blue lights shine through the flat. Another passes, then another, maybe an ambulance. All common sounds on this street, so close to the hospital and to the city centre—the soundtrack to my life.

I read the note: If you've got this, there's still time. Finish it and call. You've got the number. Don't mess up… It's hard not to look over my shoulder as I read the words. Like I'm being watched, and like the Welsh contingency posted it here in person. Like they'd driven ahead of me, found out where I lived and left it. But why not just take Sean out? They must know he's here too? Or is there another player or two in all this?

I discard all thoughts—they can wait. I know what I need to do. I'm going to take down China Bob as he meets Sean then throttle the whereabouts of Cherry, living or dead, out of Sean's limp body if I have to. I'll wring it out of him like the last drop of beer in the world from a table mat.

I ease out of my flat, down the stairs and head to an old Victorian public toilet that's opposite the flats and the petrol station on Park Row. I take the big brick of a phone there. I'll need it to summon the rabble of Welsh criminals when the time is right—but not now. I plant it behind one of the toilet bowls and if it isn't noticed, soiled, stolen, or soaked in piss later on, I'd use it to hail the storm down on us one way or another.

The beautiful old toilet block is empty, not a soul but me, and I'm in and out. With the phone there, and the drugs taped under Sean's table I'm set. Time for a drink. There's always time for a drink. I crash into the White Harte, which is too close a distraction. The doors feel and sound like echoes of a saloon in a western and in my head that suits what's unfolding. I'm the pale rider; outnumbered, outgunned, but underestimated and about to bring the shit storm to town.

Paul Benjamin, author and scribbler, sits in his usual spot. I hand him my notebook and walk to the bar and start to think he'll be a good one to ring the alarm from the mobile in the toilets, if he's got the balls or intrigue for a real story.

'Been busy, John?' he says as I return with a drink for me, but nothing for him.

'Like you wouldn't believe.'

'This story here—dark, drunken ramblings a lot of it,' he

says, flicking through my notes. 'It's okay you know. You could do something with it,' he continues, but I stay focussed on the matter at hand. I take the notebook back from him.

'This is not for you, not yet, although you could play a part, if you want to?' I ask calmly, tapping his table with it then wrapping the elastic around and pocketing it, like a gun into a shoulder holster.

'Interesting—I haven't graced my pages with anything of you I'm afraid. Gonzo's not my style.'

'Just listen,' and my eyes tighten with the seriousness of my voice, freezing his academic bodily outset to the seat. This is the real world now; he can run and stay out of it for good, but part of him wants something more tangible than the invented detective prose he's been stewing over in here, I know it.

All the time he's been pretending to himself to be a writer, making an occasional note without any reality to fuel it and flesh out its bones. And now, as he's sat in front of me, he sees the meat—dripping hard words of truth, tantalising sinews of my real trepidations and he sees the lucidity of it all and he isn't going to run and waste a chance to touch it. He wants it and he doesn't know what it is yet. Just a taste of something solid he can use in his blessed book, to make good the pretensions of it all; dirty up his words enough to make them believable.

'Listen,' I bark, and the word has him gripped. He leans on the table like he's taking communion; wafer, wine and pat on the head. I go on, 'Listen and listen good. What time does this place kick out? Eleven, eleven-thirty? Doesn't matter. There's a public toilet over there. Think they lock it at midnight. If I'm not back here by ten-thirty, I want you to go over there to the shitters, take the stall on the right…'

'Hang on!' He protests a little at the suggestion of some late-night seedy encounter.

'Not that! Listen, fuck. I don't have long—until the end of this pint in fact.' And I down it, all but a mouthful. 'Take the stall on the right. And behind the bog, there's an old mobile phone. Big brick of a thing. You can't miss it.'

'Yes.'

'Take it and call the saved number in it. Won't be hard—there's only one number in there. Call at...' and I look at the clock behind the bar that reads 20:00. 'Call the saved number at about eleven and tell whoever answers, 'He's ready for the pickup.' Do that, then call the police!'

'When they ask... where's it to?' he asks.

'Finally blending in, picking up the language are we?' I remark at his accidental slip of a Brissle tongue. 'Tell them all to go to 2 Lower Park Row—third floor—and don't bother knocking!'

And I stand slowly, drink the mouthful that's left, and leave. The set piece was in place and I felt charitable at having added some mystery and intrigue to his life. I'd hopefully see him again later and fuel his prose some more.

As I stumble on down Park Street the roads and streets strain like bulging veins, feeding the city its nightlife of office workers and revellers. Careless of what night of the week it is they spill in and out of doorways, heading from hole to hole and aiming for the inevitable waterfront bars. As I pass a bar on the left someone is thrown out by two burly bouncers. As if all orchestrated and a timed piece, another person outside the place is being sick on the pavement and into gutter. As the evicted punter turns to protest, and demand re-entry to join their office pals, they slip in the sick and fall over. They slip and slide away trying to get up but their own drunkenness, the sick on the floor and the incline of Park Street has them up and down getting more and more covered in the soup of someone else's dinner.

I pass by and a skateboarder whizzes past taking advantage of the hill's gravity. Another passes me and I find myself hoping they both fall.

I lick and roll a cigarette which is lit by the time I reach the old steps at the bottom of the street. Its two-hundred-year-old flights of steps, already drenched in revellers' piss, lead to Frogmore Street below, as Park Street bridges over it. I teeter down best I can to avoid the spills, pools and matter. And then I can see it, a hundred yards away, if that: the Hatchet Inn—one of many old Tudor-looking, higgledy-piggledy boozers that claims to be the oldest in the city, possibly one of the oldest in the county.

It used to have a rat pit to the back which it takes great delight in savouring on the occasional printout on its uneven nicotine-stained walls. The door is claimed to be made of human skin and to have been painted over time and time again throughout the centuries so is now a heavy, looming, hinged monolith. A sinister black mass, I push it open and enter the Mecca for bikers and gig-goers aiming for the ice rink building opposite. I decide it's a perfect place for me to collect myself before I push on, justifying another drink and a soak in the echoes of rat baiting and biker bravado before I tool up and head to the Bierkeller to get Sean and China Bob.

I'd soak it in, the ferocity of it all and summon my own inner gods of drink and brawl—the Viking. I didn't want to be too early into the club and get sussed by China Bob or Sean before they'd met. So, now there is time to kill and later there'll be time to kill or be killed.

It's dark and dank, stinking of stale beer and biker's gas. The giant black, bobbled human-skin door seals me, them and the stench inside like the filthy womb it is. I squeeze through the mass of leather, black tattoos, fishnets and studs that fill the place wall to wall. There must be some old punk or rock gig going on in the venue opposite or upstairs later as there's an air of drinking fast, preloading before a melee and a mosh pit. You can taste the excitement, that and all the stale beer, smoke and whatever they've eaten for lunch, which now taints the air I breathe. I squeeze through to the bar unnoticed.

I'm wearing enough black and covered in enough ominous stains to pass for one of them, or homeless. The barmaid masters the bar with an invisible might, and the closer she gets you can just sense she's the ruler here—the landlady, lion tamer and in control. She's a timeless beauty, in her later years but has lost nothing, instead made more beautiful with each passing day's wisdom, and with each biker that she's told to back off and wind their neck in if they wanted serving next, or at all. I tread respectfully, look at the pumps and order quickly and assertively to save her time in amongst the pushing and shoving of leather, BO, and bravado.

'Pint of Celtic Warrior please.'

'Okay,' she says, pulling a glass from underneath the bar and filling it at the tap whilst already spying the next in line to be served in amongst the rabble. I take the pint, squeeze out of the queue and look for a spot to drink and spy at her and admire her style.

With all the standing, queuing and shoving, I'm surprised to see a round table and two stools by the window, at the end of the bar. A notice on the wall talks of the history of the place, the ratting, the door of blood and skin and Long John Silver. Every pub in Bristol, old and young, claims some stake in the Treasure Island legacy; that and slavery. They're all adopted histories, pasts or a tale or two to bring in the punters, tourists and the bus loads of Chinese with their cameras.

A tea-stained old poster talks of the rat pit, Jack Black the old rat catcher from Victorian times and Billy. Billy was a celebrated rat killing dog, circa 1823. The poster boasts and revels in descriptions of Billy's record number of kills, the raticide and of the ringleader's pomp and ceremony with the hero's head, Billy's head, covered in gore. As if to finish the story on a sentimental note it has a swift line to say: Unfortunately, despite being a glorious and dextrous animal, he is what the French Monsieurs call Borgne: that is blind of an eye! This precious organ was lost to him some time ago by the intrepidity of an inimical rat which he had not seized in a proper place.

It makes me think on about scrapping and the set-to I have ahead of me. Will China Bob be my inimical rat, or worse?

'Ay up—looking at Billy are we?' The landlady stands in front of my table, picks up my empty glass and, as I look at her and the pub around us, I can see it's all cleared—it's just the two of us now.

'Billy and the rat pit,' I answer and look back at the poster on the wall. In words unspoken, her confidence and her correct assumption that it's okay, she pours herself and me another glass. Hers is a large whiskey and she sits down with me at the table. I move round so she's still facing the bar and able to survey her domain, like the lioness she is.

'Bit of a scrapper too are we?' And she looks me up and down, accompanied by a cheeky glimmer behind the eyes, with a slightly upturned corner of the lips, all delivered with an effortless class. Strength and sensuality, through and through— what every honourable man would wish for in a wife-to-be. She was hard not to love instantly.

'Scrape or two recently… yes. A savage birthday gift from life all just for me. Came wrapped in pure shite!'

'Happy Birthday then, scrapper,' she says, toasting my glass with a chink and a wink. 'Nothing you can't handle, or wasn't deserving though, I bet,' and with another slow wink, and a small kiss blown this time. 'You probably went out looking for it, didn't you?'

'If we stop doing what we're meant for... well we just stop, don't we?' I admit to her, and myself, out loud.

'Billy the ratter was thrown in a pit with hundreds, thousands of them. Always came out the winner. Limp little brown bodies laid everywhere. They used to put what was left on the table, hit them on the head with a stick to make sure and check they were done,' she says, looking over my head behind me as if the historical rat pit was still there. She looks out and past me into history, savouring it all as much as I am; beast against beast and the brutality and pure honesty of it.

'Long night was it? Where'd they all go?' I ask, and my words appear to change the subject, despite my mind, me and her definitely being firmly fixed in the grime of the rat baiting pit. Even as she replies, I can tell she's still summing me up and feeling it all herself too.

'They've gone opposite. King Kurt playing or some other psychobilly. I always take the hard shifts. I can't do it to the others. What's hard to me is nigh on impossible to them, anyway. I've wrestled my fair share of bikers out the door. They don't fight me back like they do the others—they know I've been, seen and done it all before!'

She looks back at the bar, and over my head, behind the bar, above the optics, dusty tankards and hundreds of beer mats stuck up with tack and yellowing tape, is an old vintage art-deco poster, the kind of three-colour print used to promote coffee shops and Moulin Rouge types in Paris. I squint my eyes to see closer, read the words and look at the body of a beautiful silhouetted girl against a large ballroom background complete with chandeliers and high ceiling.

'Twas over there, before they changed it to an ice rink and gig venue. Big huge gorgeous ballroom. Suits would come from all over—Cardiff, Birmingham, Manchester. They'd come in waves and droves of bus loads just to look at my tits,' and she cracks up, giggling and chest jiggling on the seat in front of me.

My eyes widen as I recognise the girl on the poster—it's her—and I'm in love. I smile and read the poster out loud to the dank empty pub, me, her and the smell the bikers left behind: 'Mademoiselle Pamplemousse, Coming Tonight for your pleasure and entertainment. 8pm Till Late, May 28th 1976. The South West Showcase! Courtesy of E L Noire.'

I put my eyes back in my head, refocus and look back at her in respect, love and awe.

'I know how they feel—the bikers. You've got me wrapped around your little finger,' and I nod a mini-bow over the table at her, submitting to everything she is and deserves, which is undoubtedly forever more than me.

'This isn't my day job. I've run the pub since I stopped twirling tassels for tenners, took it over about twenty years ago. I do the evening shifts. I like the characters, keeps me alive!'

'What's the day job then?'

'I read, write a little. I read others' work mainly now though. I seem to have the knack for smelling out those words that stick and sting people—real, gritty, and dirty old stuff often. Some of the publishers and other agents like it because they can often buy it cheap to sell it. I like it because I can bathe in the moments and the richness of whatever I can find in other people's lives they deem worth sharing. Looking for former glories of mine maybe, dunno—something to do isn't it. And we can't stop what we're meant to do can we? Or we just stop,' and she smiles the words at me.

'No lives can be compared to your own I'm sure. You should

write yourself out—I'd buy a copy of that…'

'What makes you think I haven't,' and she winks again with tits jiggling along to her little laugh too. Then she stands and goes over to serve a lone customer that's entered the bar behind me. I need a piss and, as I stand, I can see in the reflection of the glass behind where she was sat that the character being served is skinny and slight of frame. A loner in here—it's a hard place to drink alone and at an odd time unless your building up to, hiding from or waiting for something—like the bikers, myself and rat baiters of the past.

I stand, taking in the full reflection and walk around the corner to the urinals. As I piss, I play it back in my head; the reflection. The outline of the person, the manner, posture and gestures, all caught in the brief moments as I rose from the seat. I play it back again, and again. I know it's China Bob. He's here to preload and soak up the fighting spirit, just like me—the fucker that he is, just like me.

I tense up. I shake off, zip up, and look in the mirror. Its rust shows from the back, screw heads poking through, and there are brown stains and streaks that could be this afternoon's rockers' shit or dried-on blood from yesterday. I look hard into the dark pits of my own hard eyes. The Viking flashes before me in my irises.

This wasn't the time I had in mind for this particular confrontation with Bob, but if it came to it I'd rise up to it and get it done. Would he know me though, China Bob? I'd heard of his reputation, which had travelled ahead of him between cities. I'd heard of him breaking men here in Bristol when I was working the Hacienda doors in Manchester. If I had ever emanated any reputation or story of my case, it would have been when I testified against the Mr Bigs of Manchester. I was possibly still protected from it all by the witness protection. He won't have seen any photos of me... and the name John Barrie would mean nothing to him. It's only just starting to mean something to me, a paper mask at best. For now I might be undercover, cloaked in booze and anonymity; just a random drunk chatting up the landlady when he walked in. I can be that again if it suits me.

In a moment's flash I consider whether that life, the one of the anonymous drunk, would be any better than this, the life of the random drunk chatting up the landlady—who also happens to be a literary agent. Maybe Paul Benjamin was right in the White Harte, maybe my notebook had something and I should show her my white Moleskine now, and drop out of all this PI nonsense that's going to get me, or someone else, killed...

And then I think of Cherry, the blood up the walls in her and Sean's flat, then I'm back in the room; that of the piss- and blood-stained WCs of the Hatchet Inn. The memories of Cherry's blood on the flat wall cross-fades over the bloodstains on the mirror in front of me, those that were smacked or smeared into place from a fist or hand touching the pane after being held to a bloody nose. Clumsy smears of a drunk or belligerent, not like the flashes in the flat from a strike of a hand across a girl's face, hit with force, vigour and determined damage in mind. I'm back in the room alright—on track and on the case.

I open the toilet door and step out, my internal fire re-stoked, ready to face my demons, fight if need be and win. I'm raging, focused like a jungle warrior after his second bowl of tiger-cock soup.

I round the corner from the WCs and he's there, having taken the seat the landlady was warming up previously. He's sat as bold as brass, back to me—I think for a second whether to smash a chair over the back of his head, but fair play and wanting to hear his piece wins out over callous one-upmanship. I want to know if he knows who I am or not, and suss out my game for later. I want to see if I should just pack it all in and drop out to fight another day.

He's dressed in black too, T-shirt rolled up enough to expose the skinny taut arms. Idiots on the street and common brawlers could and probably did often confuse his slight frame with some kind of underfed waif, but I know different, I've seen it before—fatless, trim and trained, flexible muscles. Real meat, not the pumped-up empty mass from a gym vanity project, but the kind that gives dangerous mechanical advantage to the owner of the limbs that carry it and the fists on the end of them.

He was trained properly at first, then probably ran out of dojos or got banned from one. Someone maybe lost an eye or worse—just like Billy the ratter. China Bob was a big rat and for now I could see straight with both my eyes in their sockets and I'm thinking twice about joining him at the table—but I do.

My legs are already walking to the table by the time my mind has caught up and committed itself. It was on now: the game's cards are in hand, dealer dealing the table with another one or two to the green, and we're all just sitting it out for now, scoping the terrain and analysing the eyes of the other players—who has what, who's making the first move, and what will happen next. I'm in, I decide. I walk over and sit down opposite him.

24

Outside the weather had decided to turn and rip into the side of the old Tudor-looking pub; inside another storm brewed as we sat opposite each other. Whereas, the elements outside hadn't held back and had come with the full force of nature, inside, the tornados of our true being were kept bottled up for now, neither man exposing his real meaning or the point of his being there in this dank stinking bar.

Two pints appeared as the table refreshed itself, helped by E L Noire—Mademoiselle Pamplemousse, the burlesque table centrepiece. I sit looking into his cold, dead, robotic stare where there is nothing, not a glimmer, scent or essence of humanity. As I look into him, in turn, my heartbeat shrinks to barely a pulse and my own stony-faced silence and demeanour starts to mirror his.

Out of the corner of an eye, as I hold my gaze forward at Bob, protecting my guard, as I'm unsure if I might end up with a glass smashed in my face if I do look away, in my peripheral vision ,I notice a flash of black and flesh, like a crow's wings, and am reminded of the girl I found asleep in the back of the car. I think on as to whether I'm to be constantly haunted now by these colourful characters: a vain Irishman, Cherry, the Bear, the hard, old Governor, the girl with them, Paul Benjamin the writer, and this nut and nut-cracker that's in front of me now—

China Bob.

And… in a moment's breath I concede my life is better with them all in it, with more colour and vibrancy, with my whole outlook having been, only a few days ago, just that of black and white—a dull grey haze.

My stomach rumbles, and I feel my innards turn over; half in excitement, half with constrained, strangled nerves as I fight to control my calm. They turn over again, more determined this time and the bubble of wind is uncertain to me. Harmless gas or a risk I might shit myself and show my nerves, hand and true colours; despite my, up until now, Zen-like control. Stuck locked in a stare with the deadly street-brawling killer, I hold it all in despite knowing the sure ice-breaking qualities of a disowned fart, smelled but unheard.

Like two poised cobras before the strike we wait and then it comes; calm, calculated and more threatening than any blow— the words of one killer to another. As he starts to quote the bloody outcome from a ratting history from the old notice on the wall by us—I know he knows about me, or I can't afford not to think so for now. I know he's about to talk about us and the fight to come really, it's a test of my guilty conscience, If I've something to hide; my strength and my commitment. It's a clever test and not least because it challenges my identity for both himself and for me. How far will I go? Am I prepared to go all the way?

The storm stops outside and, with what seems like the endless trickle of a raindrop down the window pane, the dark energies and turmoil are transferred seamlessly inside the room on his words as they leave his lips. His mouth moves with minimum effort, lips like a paper cut opening just far enough to let the slightest air carrying the words escape. Vehemence and viciousness masked in whispered paraphrasing. I could tell the seriousness by his lack of outward effort, which I had so far looked to match, not giving anything away or confirming my place in this orchestra noir, complete with table dancer, drinks and entertainment. Now it was time for the bitter interlude before the inevitable main act. I just needed to see it through and survive.

I down half the pint on the table that has rested to have half a reasonable head, and I settle in for his test and storytelling, all whilst listening out for the layers of interrogation and analysis I assume would be there for me. I keep my senses on alert for what could all be just an obvious distraction before a physical assault. I'm transfixed, poised and hypnotised by the moment... waiting for each word to drop from his slit of a mouth.

'Billy, the famous dog-ratter would kill one hundred rats in one minute. One minute...' he hisses. Picking the words out from the notice on the wall, layering them with the fierce subtext between us, 'A hundred of them, bodies made limp by the snap of his jaw. Calmest and most efficient way, that way. One bite—done.' And he looks at my hands on the table; a look for a tremble, a tell sign or a fidget. I feign interest by holding his gaze and reach in my pocket for my papers and tobacco pouch. My hand brushes past my white notebook and it throbs at me like a beating heart sucking in the energies between us. 'Their mangled corpses,' he slowly goes on at me, 'the corpses that would prove valour for the victor. A heap of flesh, fur and shattered bone.'

'Lost an eye, did Billy,' I say and throw a rolled cigarette at him and start to roll another for myself. 'Didn't see one rat coming, did he? And was forever left not quite able to see the rest coming. There's always a bigger rat—retired him from duty in the end.'

'Bite, tear, rip into the flesh. A broken killer... Billy.' China Bob's eyes flare up as he puts the rolled cigarette slowly up to his lips and his hands move under the table. 'Are you a killer? No? Maybe? Let me see, let's look at you,' and his focus tightens.

But I'm nothing, I'm stone, I'm a ghost and I'm a cold demon. I am a killer, been killed myself and reborn and he can smell parts of it lingering, I'm sure.

His nostrils flare to match his focus, 'Yes, let me see… I can't see anything.'

His words are mocking, a provocation to see if I'll push back or give anything away. I realise this isn't a test of identity any more but a test of strength; a show of teeth, a comparison of scars, a bitch and bravado to the wind. It means nothing to me, I'm made of stone.

'Maybe you are, just maybe,' he continues with fag hanging now in his tight lips. 'I've seen the look, your look—I see it every day in the mirror. You are a killer. You can do it can't you—hit, bray, and batter a man, fucking bite! You can do it and you've seen it too, that other look, the one of defeat. Not knowing if it'll end for them, and them so fucked up they half-wish it would, that you'd just finish them for good and end it. The pain. You ever got a man down like that?' he whispers.

I stay cold and calm, lift my now rolled cigarette to my lips and gesture for him to finish.

'Ever got him down, surrendered, in his hell? The one you've made for him, carved out of terror?'

'He'll let you tie his hair in bunches, rut him, call him Gina if you want… if that's your thing?' I return fire with a slight smile and words testing his bravado at the questioning of his sexuality. A joke to me, too close to the bone maybe for him. Either way it showed my calm and resolve.

I realise his hands are still under the table. The air in the rooms stops. E L Noire's hands pause on the pump she's been cleaning provocatively, and the music, if there was any, also quits for a moment, like a hanky in mid-air before the drop of a guillotine. He doesn't smile; his eyes sharpen even more into dots, and although I can't see them I know his teeth are clenching because the muscles show through the tightened flesh of his cheeks. I see his arms move slightly as his hands move under the table, clasping and gripping something...

CLICK! The noise echoes about the room. The cocking of a gun or the flicking of a knife, so distinct a sound...

CLICK! His hands both move slowly to the table top and his right extends as he lights my fag with his matt-black Zippo, the source of the noise, flickering in the air in front of me as I remain unchanged—stone, all but for a bead of sweat down the hackled hairs in the centre of my back.

I inhale deeply, exhale, down my pint, stand to leave, and I fart—a quiet bodily escape for a pub, not so quiet for this moment, on a knife edge. As I stand in the corner of the room, I glimpse to see the girl in the corner, the one from the car I'd found asleep in the short black dress. She's been sat watching us all this time. I walk slowly away towards the exit.

'What did you say your name was again?' China Bob asks to my back.

'I didn't,' I say, and continue walking out. Before the door made of blood and skin closes behind me, I can hear the music start up again, a chink of glass from the bar and Mademoiselle Pamplemousse...

'Did one of you let one go?' she chuckles, sensing the imbalance of male hormone in the room, and she adjusts and retakes ownership of the place immediately with a single comment. She has power over her domain. An easy one to love.

Despite my cornered-skunk of an exit from the place, I feel as though I've got out safely: unscathed, alive and having tested the field for later as well as having saved face. The exchange pointed towards Bob, a repressed homosexual or not, definitely wanting to be respected as a top dog and to put on a show. Maybe having gone a while without a challenge, now he finds entertainment in the theatre of each new conflict, both the entertainment inherent in it, and that which he can create for his own amusement.

What remains of the evening's rain drips from the rooftops as I walk from Frogmore Street past the strip bars behind the theatre and the smell of fish, chips and vinegar that stings my nose. The stink makes me gag a little, and then increases to a lot as I pass between the entrance to the chip shop that's opposite the strip joint. The smell from each is undistinguishable as separate, blending to a fish soup of a stench hanging in the air—without doubt neither source of the reek is actually edible.

I walk across the grass of the city centre and up through the historic four, five and six-storey buildings of Corn Street and Bristol's banking past. The copper nails in the street at the top stand testament to countless deals done, twisted and forced by the city's trades with and without slavery. Bitter pasts, selectively remembered for tourist trails, but masked every day and forgotten, replaced by historical traders in spice if it helps the city sleep at night.

Drunks, hens and stags are at it again. Feathers from boas scattered everywhere and I wonder when the bubble will burst and the 90s, like the 80s, will break, dip. Or if these people's livers will do so first, as they make every night look like a Saturday.

I look at my watch, which says nothing, and decide on another drink to settle the nerves, recollect myself after the near bashing and face off with China Bob. I want to make a note or two in the white notebook that was figuring out, predicting and recording events as well as my defined self. It had started as a blank canvas, like me, and had grown into its new identity with each note and slice of this story as it unfolded. And so I rebound from one bikers' pub to another, into The Crown to make my last peace before the inevitable confrontation with Sean the Bastard to find out what he's done with Cherry; all if I can get past, outfox or distract Bob again—although I may be out of wind by then.

The Crown hadn't changed and would never change. It was how pubs used to be before the 80s and 90s happened. Not an obvious briefcase or Chelsea pinstripe in sight. It had evolved and sprung up in a less obvious part of town hundreds of years ago, like a spring for weary travellers, bikers and shoppers in the side streets of the old market, down a paved narrow walkway— and long may it last.

In between the punks, Mohicans, green hair, studs and tattoos, are goths and, if you look even closer, not getting distracted by the more colourful interesting elements, you can see the outcasts, office workers, writers, street thieves and market workers—them and me, hiding in the shadows, sat at tables in the corners or leaning against the bar. My faded shade of dirty black fits seamlessly into another place and I find my perch and sit it out with another drink or three.

The music is loud and so is the crowd—another leather-clad rabble, most of it. Despite its outward appearance there was never a fight in The Crown, possibly because, like the wallpaper and toilet roll, the beer prices hadn't been changed in ten years. The biker clientele exuded a more hippy outlook, inclusive and welcoming of each other and new people with a grunt and a shove—and I got mine too. It felt good to belong to a crowd for a while. I suspect Zen and the Art of Motorcycle Maintenance was among an unspoken reading list.

Welcomed, watered, and seated, I waited my time and took

it all in—my predicament and duty going forward.

I didn't want to head to the Bierkeller too soon ahead of China Bob, only for him to come up behind me and fuck me over. And who was the girl from the car back seat who also was sitting watching over the proceedings in the Hatchet? Is she friend, foe or a blood-eyed spectator like those of the old ratting pits?

I obviously either wasn't hard to track, or China Bob and I share the same interests and patterns... Upon pondering our possible common paths, I look around, quickly surveying the room—nothing, and no out-of-place, skimpy black cocktail dress either. I just hope Paul Benjamin, the struggling writer and scribbler, comes through on his part—makes the call.

If I can get to the Bierkeller, beat the whereabouts of Cherry's body—if that's all that's left—out of Sean, and then point him towards the flat for his drugs, money and my shit, then I can put him to bed. If Paul Benjamin comes through, makes the call to the other rabble—Bear, Bitch, Governor and Cherry's other lover—then they can all get in the bed they've made for themselves and the final call to the police will settle it for good: case closed. China Bob was a spanner in the works, maybe, a tough nut and robotic killer without a conscience in the mix. Although to all these players, so was I.

I complete my notes, recording the crazed events to date one frenzied scribble at a time, then I snap the notebook shut, stretch the elastic around the thoughts inside; thoughts of me and my time in this new skin I wear.

I look down at my hands holding the chewed biro pen. Although my writing has been manic it's still legible and my hands are still calm and surging with the battles of my yesterdays. I had survived them all and the ones more recently, self-imposed; the trial by fire; and the swim out to sea. My beer-rotten soul had embraced the Viking of my past. I clench my fists so tight that the white of my knuckles pushes through to the skin like snooker balls. My body tenses, shaking as AC/DC blasts out the soundtrack to my moment from the juke box, rattling pint glasses on the tables around me.

The image of the room's punks and bikers slows to a blurred cloud around me. Motion blurs follow each of them—their hair, studs and tattoos trailing before my eyes. My head drops, my eyes close and slowly open back up again and he's there opposite me again—the Viking.

'Crazy...' he says in a softly spoken Scottish tone. 'You're fucking crazy, man!'

'Who isn't?'

'Yeah, man, who isn't? Writing notes, scribbling away to yourself. Yar nutter,' and he points at the notebook on the table top, in a small pool of lager and ash. 'Lost in your world of words, and blaming other people in the situations they describe. Writing to yourself—bat-shit crazy, man, bat-shit!'

'One person's crazy is another one's sane—we're all on the scale,' and as the words leave my lips I see his image falter, shimmering away from being my alter ego and strength. He looks enough like the Viking to pull it off but my brain and imagination has filled in the gaps around it, making it real to me—he's just another beer-drunk crazy in here. Just like me... I smile and he smiles back. We share a cigarette I've rolled, and I hand him a bonus fake fifty I've found in my pocket and tell him to enjoy his night.

'I will, I will. But remember, son... that won't help...

you can't drink away your past!' he says, sucking the last life out of the cigarette and letting it drop into my near empty pint glass. He stands and goes straight to the bar, up the half flight of stairs behind me, and I hear a cheer sounding like I've just sponsored him and his pals' drinks for the night. That or I've just made a whore out of the barmaid and he's stuck it down her top—I've made him a superstar amongst drunk bikers.

Out of the pub and back on the street by the pub picnic tables, I stop, I breathe and I think: Are you sure you're meant for this, PI John Barrie? Is this your style? The name you're sticking with for now? Are you going to see this through?

A flash of black and legs and dress flaps past the end of the alley and something tells me it's too late to get out of this whole escapade. And when all is said and done, what did that fuck do to Cherry? The blood up the wall, the hastily emptied wardrobe... What did he do? And why?

I know the whys, or pretty much—he didn't like her choice of second boyfriend or lover, his customer across the bridge; that and the guy across the bridge was a better version of him, drug dealer or not. More depth to him from what I saw. I may be biased because of the shared past in the services but it's all part of it. Sean, well he's just paper thin and a meagre small dog turd, waiting to be washed away by the rain. No lasting impression other than getting stuck on a shoe for a while.

As the thoughts mill around my boozed-up and battered brain, my mind wanders to my dream where I was on Brandon Hill. Where Cherry was the young girl from the Banksy graffiti, carrying a red balloon. I imagine that she stops her walk with me across the park and says, 'Eew, I trod in something.'

'Don't worry. Shit comes and goes, doesn't last... never does,' I say to her, and we giggle and walk off in the direction of the ice cream truck that's still playing some carnival, instrumental version of Rage Against the Machine's 'Killing In the Name'.

'Fuck you, I won't do what you tell me,' she giggles, singing along, skipping, happy, and safe as she's holding my hand.

The bump and shove of a punk getting past me snaps me back into the reality of the alleyway and what was at hand for me to do.

'I'm coming for you, Sean. China Bob… Cherry,' and I put up the collar on my coat, take a half-finished fag out of the nearby ashtray, draw on it and walk into the night, armed only with my blood, guts and heart. Same as I'd taken into any battle, only this time I care for the outcome

It was beyond any imposed politic or will of a machine. The situation was a random mix of real life, the fire and blood that I'd been a part of stoking up, and now I was going to put it out for good. I'd put it out and move on to the next draft of my new identity, puzzle to solve, case to break.

25

I stop at the end of the old alleyway which has The Crown on it. A version of 'Dirty Old Town' is playing from a nearby Irish pub, from which drunken patrons spill out with the light from inside onto the cobbles outside. It draws me instantly, influencing my decision to turn right, in the wrong direction, and move towards the fiddle playing and the Guinness, rather than the left turn that would lead more efficiently towards the Bierkeller, and my looming confrontations.

Drunks in caps stumble to and fro. Pints spill and fags teeter in mouths as if they could be forgotten and might drop to the cobbles any moment. It's a good honest scene of love and life. No pretensions and with the song to match in the background, not like the shit the waterfront bars are playing at this same time in the night.

Opposite the entrance to Seamus O'Donnell's there's an old drinking fountain from the 1700s—overly ornate, almost Catholic in appearance. Maybe it was, in fact, a gift from the Church long ago but now it's just used as an empty can and pint glass drop.

A bleached white-headed sculpture of a queen mounts the top of it with stark ruby-red lips. Above the head someone has scribbled in chalk, with a line projecting from the queen's mouth as if she's preaching the words at me herself… I wonder if it's another cryptic message, meant for me. Maybe it's been left by the young girl that seems to be stalking, flashing and fleeting about me, the nearer I get to my cause. How could she have known I would turn right at the end of the alley though? Or maybe I'd taken an unexpected route to The Crown in the first place and this was meant to be seen before that?

Predicting the route of drunk isn't as complex as she may have made it for herself; she should have just written on the door of one or two of the inhabitable drinking holes between the White Harte, Hatchet Inn and the Bierkeller.

Possibly this message between The Crown and the Irish pub was planted here with just that in mind though; the same rationale… I stop by the drunks, and read it to myself as the rain starts up and seems to wash away each line as I'm reading.

Write what you see, not what you think you see—facts.

Use words to say what you feel, not what you imagine people want to read.

Be honest, brutal and raw. It makes it all believable—the truth is harder to ignore.

Be real.

Piss, shit, fuck, and get caught short like anyone else… eat if you absolutely have to, likewise with sleep—unless it's a really interesting and relevant dream.

A passing writer's note. RIP Chinaski. 9.3.94

Like a gambler with a habit, a drunk, a wife-beater and an idiot, I see self-justification and reaffirmation of my purpose in each line I've just read, before the rain eventually washes it to the floor and the liquid chalk dusts my feet.

I stand a while, then my heels scrape the cobbles as I about-turn, walk straight into the Irish bar, and order a pint of Mother's Milk: a Guinness.

26

The queue for the entrance to the Bierkeller is down another piss-riddled street, this one winding down from Castle Park and the market streets above. Bristol City centre's hills have confused many a drunk, but now they act in my favour, working with gravity to pull me down into the pit that is Broadmead.

Remnants of rain and urine wash down the fag butts with The Pithay into the feet of the goths, wasters, rockers, grunge layabouts and students of all breeds, the security guards and then me. The smoke and music bellow out from inside, bass vibrating cars on the streets around us. A distant car alarm is set off and joins in, almost in tempo.

I try to keep low key, under the radar of security. Having worked that role, I know nothing really escapes them if they're any good. I'm alone, five or ten years older than the rest of the queue and carry the marks of someone who's been beaten, slept rough and steamrollered recently. Other than the age I could have pulled off some sort of grunge, goth thing in appearance.

As I stand, my confident demeanour, tired and covered in the shit of a well-worn-in-pair-of-shoes life, I look like I must actually be staff; fucked over, underpaid and having seen, felt and delivered a beating or ten in the past.

No sooner do I realise that I'm sticking out and so out of place, then I'm plucked from the queue by a bomber-jacketed mule, one I really don't want to get kicked by.

'You're in,' he states, looking me up and down, and drags me by my shoulder up to the front of the queue, in through the double doors and past the paying-in booth. He then uses my entire body to point me up the stairs leading to the core and the roar coming from the place.

Carpeted steps and posters line the way and each poster has a z or x replacing an s as if to confirm its rock or metal credentials. The stairs sweep up round to the right, and the room opens up to a large bar on the left, packed with another huddle of black-clad shovers, and pool tables with heroin-chic young girls using them as benches.

Steps lead down to the main event, which was currently looking like a Filipino taxi dance hall, complete with factions waiting on either side in the shadows and on tables and seats; waiting for the song which would meet their approval or a prospective partner's on the opposite side of the room. Approval by both in a song good enough to entice them both down to mosh together, shoe gaze, step, slide or just wig out like Ian Curtis fitting to a strobe.

I make a cursory scan of the room as smoke and lights flood the place as I try to make out a Sean- or China Bob-shaped silhouette amongst it all. Eventually I find one of them: Sean the Bastard. He's sat like an arrogant king of the indie club at the end of one of the long tables to the left-hand side, near the dance floor. I keep my distance and try to make out how much support he might have near him.

Sweat, condensation and worse drips down every column, wall and surface. Its pores ooze every whim, touch, grab, and taken opportunity in the toilets at the back—the physical, mutual and chemical. Why clubs insist on carpet anywhere is a sticky, stinking mystery to me, not least now as I pull myself over the floor.

At least in here, the carpet ends where the dance floor starts, if you could call it that—wood patched with laminate that no one ever sees because the lights are so low and the stains so constant and varied holding it all together. I skulk successfully around the bar and perimeter. I do a shot of tequila, then another, and then I'm ready. A new song starts playing and I'm reminded of my dream, the ice cream truck and my abrupt waking to lyrics: *Untethered... Now transformed, reborn, rebuilt and remade... For some lost soul's sake!*

The song builds and I walk over, occasional strobes lighting me up like I'm a spectre being quickly switched on and off. And then I'm there, stood at the end of his table. Sean's table.

Despite the noise of the music, the smoke and the darkness with silhouettes, shadows and people massing around, I'm in a heightened state of alert. Old form and practices are awakened in me. After all, this is a club, not a war scene, and I'm not in Ireland, I'm stood here, not crawling in the dirt in a hedge and not on fire, being shot at. Yes, I'm on high alert, switched on, and can feel the room, people, and everything in it.

'Where's my gear, you t-w-a-t?' Sean barks through the darkness and over the table at me. That's all I make out from his words, the ones that aren't drowned in the sound of a wall of raging guitar around us, that is. It's like an angry, broken machine from the speakers, but most of his vent is easy enough to make out and lip read. It's all just a sad mix of desperate anger and frustration really.

'Interesting you aren't so bothered about the girl any more. Where's Cherry, you FUCK?!' He didn't need to lip read any of my response—my yell cuts through the air like a giant axe into the table he's on.

'Who gives a fuck... Where's my shit, NOW?!' and he

attempts a look of some movie hard-man. But real life isn't like the movies. The real hard men don't need to show anything. I look at his hands on the table, bruised and cut from the abuse he's imposed on her—Cherry—and a dragon awakens again in me, the fire, the Viking and all that comes with it. My stare tightens at him and he looks uncertain, scared. Like a child cornered by a rabid dog.

'Under your fucking nose, shit bag... When you next sit down at home, look under the table—idiot!' I say it to him, and the seed is planted. Enough for him to stop and think, if he can, and go put himself in place at his flat. He looks on at me... before mouthing off another round.

'You dirty fucker—that was you wasn't it? Messing up my pad?' and, as he shouts the words, he looks off to the left of where he's sat for one of his would-be soldiers to step in. Or China Bob. He'd got what he thought he needed, and now he needed me done in, distracted, and gone from his worry altogether.

I'm grabbed by separate factions by both my shoulders and pulled away from the long table where I was addressing Sean. The hands on me pull me to the dance floor, spin me round then hold my arms back where I'm pinned in front of a third character who pulls his fist back to strike. I was never much of a slugger, stylistic fighter or show-off. But I got it all done—clumsy, ugly or otherwise. The result is what mattered then, as it does now. Like a reattached limb, my blood re-pumps to once sleeping nerves, reawakening the muscle memories. The song in the background, like in the park and my dream before I awoke, is reaching its final act and crescendo:

Untethered. The song starts its end piece and I stamp hard, like a tipper truck bucket, onto the feet of the two behind who are holding my arms. I then step forward, twisting my right arm free and bringing it up to use my hand to break the fingers that hold me. They crack back with a snap that's clearly heard above the sound of the music.

Reborn. And I grab the man to my right and push him towards the man in front, whose fist is now finishing its arc at me. A strobe flashes as the fist makes contact, and a nose sprays scarlet to the patched floorboards.

Rebuilt. And I sweep the legs of the misplaced puncher then stamp down on the side of his knee, stamping through the leg, not pulling any force in the strike, which echoes another crack around the room. Spectating innocents that have gathered nearby now vomit at the reality of the violence. Not just another drunken showpiece, this was mean delivered bodily damage— the real deal. Others turkey-neck to get a closer look at the ruckus, then shield their eyes when they see too much.

...and remade. I again hit the one that's been floored by his pal's swing, to make sure his nose is broken and that he's staying down. A bottle hits me on the head and I kneel down and hold my head. I look at my hands for blood—there's nothing. I stand slowly and the strobe flashes me on and off. As I stand upright and look forward, the last flash of the lights show him in front of me: China Bob.

He's wearing the same cold, robotic empty stare. Dangerous, unpredictable. My performance so far has unrattled him. I see he was the origin of the first bottle that hit me and has a second dangling from his right hand. He then steps forward and smashes with full force over my head and I retreat into a kneeling position. He's only a step away, just in front of me as I'm bent over like a prisoner waiting on a beheading.

For a second I'm puzzled as to his use of pub brawling tactics with bottles. He uses these tools rather than his back catalogue of martial arts.

'Hello, ratter… hoped it was you in the Hatchet. And so glad you're here now,' he talks down at me, and in the space between the lines of the final lyrics of the song.

For some lost soul's sake. I take a bow, nodding at the floor and then I stand, simultaneously raising my open fist at his crotch… I grab, twist and yank hard. I pull so hard I feel a snap and a pop.

Even the most vicious of a beast has the same Achilles heel as a small puppy, and as I stand he is in tears, staring in disbelief. I brush myself down in a show of finality—that's all, folks—and I'm gone from the dance floor.

For some lost soul's sake. The words repeat, finishing the song. I look to Sean's table as I walk out and can see he's gone to his flat, the drugs, the other dealers from Wales waiting for him and his demise with the police… if Paul Benjamin has made the calls I asked him to.

I go to the park on Brandon Hill, picking up a small bottle of Jameson on the way that I wouldn't open, make a note or two in the notebook and then I sleep heavy, done and dusted on a park bench.

27

The next afternoon, when I'm back in the White Harte, Paul Benjamin looks like he's seen the devil in that old Victorian toilet I asked him to make the calls from. I can see the big brick of a thing on the table in front of him, so know he's come through and made the call... that and the sirens I saw passing the night before, and the silhouetted action that played out in the windows of the flat as I walked quietly on to the park with my whiskey. All sirens that passed that time weren't the usual ambulance traffic to and from the hospital.

I walk past him to the bar, order two drinks and make another scribble in the notebook whilst waiting for the barman to pull them. I feel I owe him a read, to fuel his own mission— his writing. My thoughts of the past few days written out there should be worth more to him than a dodgy fifty, if there's any left, or even this liquid thanks being poured now. I take it all to him, and hand it over.

'Enjoy, use or discard. You said you saw something in it last time. Keep it, it was just therapy to me,' and I put the notebook in front of him with his drink. 'Just don't turn out to be a thug from Manchester, or a dealer from Bristol or over the bridge...' He still looks shell-shocked by life and just stares out at me. He snatches at the notebook like a starving man at a fresh green apple with dew on its skin. I wonder what was so dramatic about his two calls he made for me to the police and to the gang across the bridge; maybe it's just because it was in such stark contrast to his normal everyday life imagining crime fiction; his sheltered self was jolted and forced to take a step or two into the true realities of it around him.

I look away from him as the door eases open, creaking, and a beautiful image walks in. Paul Benjamin doesn't look up as he's too engrossed in the pages of my mind, but I'm dumbfounded, gripped to the seat, and the pint slides through my fingers and hits the tabletop. My fingers are still close enough to the rim to prevent an overspill and I just catch it.

Cherry—not shy and retired, but demure and controlled—walks confidently in, looks straight at me and stops the room and everything in it like a juggernaut. She has power, grace, control and beauty—like a younger E L Noire of the Hatchet. Her hair moves with the air from outside to reveal a plaster over her eye with blood seeping through. It had been on a day or two and had dried. As I try to get my breath she sits opposite me.

'Drink—or are you still finishing that one?' she says, and I feel an explanation coming. If not I was going to insist on one. I stare, swallow, then I down the pint...

'Yes please,' and as the words struggle, mumbled from my lips, I know I'm a pathetic man... I'm a little puppet of a man in the presence of a goddess—a goddess and the grand master of this whole thing as it's been played out.

'Coming up, and don't be so hard on yourself. It was your first case, wasn't it?' And with a wry smile she goes to the bar. At the table next to me I can see Paul Benjamin is eavesdropping, reading and adding a word or two to the back of the Moleskine, which doesn't look as pure and white as it did when it started out a day or two ago. It doesn't look as blank and without a brand or identity. With the words, thoughts and events that stain its once pure sheets, it's defined and recorded its own identity—as I have now.

'So, who goes first?' she says ,with a friendly assured tone, but I'm not sure how much I've been played yet and she has so far tried to give me the feeling we're on the same side, with her dry smile, offer of a drink and going first at suggesting a clearing of the air.

The shock of her walking in has left me untrusting though and I'm closed-up and suspicious. 'Well, I guess it's me then, soldier boy.' Again she delivers the words with a wry smile and what's this suggestion of my military past? She hasn't seen my scars, my history…or has she?

'You're the fuzz,' I state plainly.

'Well done,' she says, like a teacher complimenting a primary school child, 'and…'

'Undercover?'

'Goes without saying, Columbo—look at me…'

Her sarcasm breaks the ice a little more, and I desperately want her to be onside but am blinded slightly by a superficial subconscious that looks at her like any man without a brain and just wants her. My mind wobbles off, then back on track, and works at the depth of the situation and her place in this.

'The young girl fleeting about town, following me round—one of you lot?'

'She's not that young. Doesn't drink or have kids—works wonders for the complexion you know,' Cherry says, whilst not really saying anything, and I grow impatient, change tack, provoke and prod for more pace to what was building to a slow reveal on her behalf. I want to pull the plaster off the whole situation in a quick single rip, not as slow as this tickling and pulling at each other's hair was going so far.

'Why'd you fuck him? Them both?'

'It got complicated. It got real,' she says, and I see a crack in the veneer.

'Seriously, fucking one dealer wasn't enough—you had to play them off against each other, across the bridge?' My words changed the tone of the standoff and like the situation being discussed, it got real. She looks at the table, a chink in her armour or a pause for thought before she returns fire at me, or trying to pluck the right words from the filthy tree that had become our lives now, entwined by the roots and branches of the city's underworld, street and scum that washed through it at low tide. I had maybe shoved enough now and I sat patiently as she regained composure and I waited for what was to come out of her mouth.

'I was trapped in a situation. I saw him as an out... a way of escape.'

'The Trench Coat, with the bruiser Bear and strumpet across the bridge?'

'Yes. I saw use for him against Sean... a standoff between them, one that would finish them both. And when that failed I saw use for you against them all. I was wrong about them. I was, however, right about you.'

'How did you know who I was, enough to think I would be able to do anything?'

'Someone back at the station left the right case file out on their desk when they pissed off to the pub, and left me to work a late night and fill in for them. Your case file. It made for interesting reading—seemed like too much of a coincidence you being in the same building, the floor below. You must have been listening to all the shit as I tried and failed to sort it out. You saw my eyes, John, you saw more than a hopeful glance from a neighbour when I was trapped and being dragged round by him...'

'Why did you leave the dress, that one dress in the wardrobe?'

'His favourite, dirty bastard—he can keep it. I left it as a clue to whoever opened the cupboard next… I hoped so anyway.'

'How did you know I'd survive, and stay on course?'

'I didn't… but my pal from the station was looking out for you too.'

'The young thing from the back seat…'

'You got the messages—and the one off the windscreen?' As she says it I'm immediately reminded of the ticket from the windscreen on the car, with the police tape—the car of Sean's that surely should have been clamped or stolen when I'd left it overnight in Clifton. But no, there was a young girl, a sleeping guard, in the back seat and a ticket on the windscreen.

I look over to Paul Benjamin and he opens the back pouch of the Moleskine and hands me the yellow police ticket envelope. I take it and open it. Its words are out of date but their intent make the conversation now and events that have happened seem more as if planned, orchestrated and less random.

Stay on track, John, and record everything. Write it down. We need evidence and we need them in the same room together with the blow. Stay strong, you're doing okay. Call us when it's set up.

'Good job I did.'

'I really was right about you, you know? And now you're back. On form. You're better out of protection; it'll drive someone like you mad, if you're not already… in a good way. There's a point to you now—for you to go on doing what you're designed to do!' she says, and her words are right and feel like much more of a sweet kiss coming from her. But also, they feel like a badge, a stripe or a pat on the back from a dad that was never there.

She was right and now I was untethered from the boredom of the human race, the dog machine that had restrained me, and I could operate under my own rules and correct all the ominous things I'd done before in my life for duty or a misplaced respect. One case at a time, I'd do this. I would correct time itself as I reshaped and flexed my future self.

She leaves and I'm empowered, being more touched by her than anybody or anything to date. She had confirmed my purpose, approved my true identity to move forward.

Looking over at Paul Benjamin I can see he's returned the notebook to my table and in his hand is a small white piece of card. He leans over, sombre and serious.

'I can't take your notes, it's all you, but I thank you anyway—you've opened my eyes enough already. It was right what I said to you before—there's something in it. Take this and call her!' His hand gestures to me, holding a small card, and I take it from him and turn it over. On one side in an art-deco handwritten style it says:

A stone rose to the filth and the scum of this dirty old town and on the front side:

E. L. Noire, Literary Agent

'Mademoiselle Pamplemousse,' I whisper quietly to myself, and leave.

I take the card with me and decide I'll post my notes in what was once a simple white characterless notebook to her. My new life has been shaped by one true goddess and why not hand it, written, over to another to appreciate as I move on...

And when I get an envelope to deliver it in, I'll pick up another notebook to fill. A black one this time with red elastic holding it shut like a slice through flesh.

I aim the Viking in me at Salford in Manchester to break the next case I find wide open. I'll record it all as I take the fight to them, the demons of my past. I'll wear the scars with pride as I carve out a future for me and for someone else.

ABOUT THE AUTHOR

John writes articles, poetry, reviews, short stories and novels. His fiction is a semi-autobiographical mix of dirty realism, crime fiction and noir. Ghostly references to a heritage that includes the Vikings, Scotland, Ireland and the North, flavour the words throughout. Often with a dark but humoured edge.

John's writing has appeared online and in print for the likes of Bristol Noir, Storgy Magazine, Litro Magazine, Punk Noir Magazine, Necro Magazine and Deadman's Tome.

John lives in Bristol with his wife and daughters, where he has been since the late nineties. He is a professional designer, artist and writer as well as a proud husband, father, brother and son.

In 2017 John Bowie founded BRISTOL NOIR, a popular e-zine specialising in crime and dark fiction. You can follow them at www.bristolnoir.co.uk or on twitter @NoirBristol or Instagram @noirbristol

BRISTOL NOIR

NEXT IN THE SERIES

TRANSFERENCE
LOVE + HATE IN RAIN CITY

'BRUTAL, DARK AND LYRICAL MANC NOIR'

As clubbers in Manchester's most notorious club partied hard in the 90s, a girl collapsed, falling from the stage after a bad pill.

Few noticed. Those that did, didn't care, lost in a hedonistic haze.

John Black, an ex-SAS soldier, who was working security that night, carried her out in his arms.

Now on witness protection for exposing the city's underworld after the girl's death, he returns to the city that disowned him. Helping a troubled mother search for answers to her son's suicide—as eerie recordings tell of increased sexual depravity in the block of flats he jumped from.

Confronting the orchestrator of his pains, he works to solve the case, have vengeance…and reclaim his lost identity.

'Lyrical-poetry and prose mix with blood down Manchster's harsh rain-soaked alleyways.'

Lightning Source UK Ltd.
Milton Keynes UK
UKHW040920141020
371560UK00001B/241